DRAGONTHROAT
—A NOVEL OF ALTIVA—

AIRSHIP 27 PRODUCTIONS

TM

Dragonthroat (A novel of Altiva)
© 2021 Teel James Glenn

Published by Airship 27 Productions
www.airship27.com
www.airship27hangar.com

Interior illustrations © 2021 Chris Nye
Cover illustration © Rob Davis

Editor: Ron Fortier
Associate Editor: Fred Adams Jr.
Marketing and Promotions Manager: Michael Vance
Production designer: Rob Davis

ISBN: 978-1-953589-16-3

Printed in the United States of America

10 9 8 7 6 5 4 3 2 1

DRAGONTHROAT
—A NOVEL OF ALTIVA—

BY TEEL JAMES GLENN

Chapter One

That day in 1985 was perhaps the strangest day in T.K. Mitchell's singularly strange life yet it began pleasantly, as so many others had, with a slight hangover and a beautiful woman beside him.

Things went downhill from there; by nightfall, he was running for his life with the woman's brothers trying to blow his brains out.

Fortunately for all concerned they were terrible shots.

Sometime later Mitchell reflected on that particular turn of luck to a fellow passenger on an Amtrak train. "Whitefawn and I headed out cross-country 'til I hit that whistle stop this train came through. Damn lucky I made it; I was pretty much done in and could not have gone much farther."

He was seated in the rear-facing seat on a passenger train, his sneakered feet resting on the seat opposite him and his well-worn backpack and frame on the seat beside him.

"It all seems so very sordid, young man," the woman passenger said. She was grey-haired with sharp features and dressed in a plain grey, almost featureless dress. Her piercing, dark eyes seemed to judge him to be very lacking but he shrugged.

"Well, not all that much, really," Mitchell said in a gravel voice. "Her brothers were bigots who took a dislike to me—my pretensions of being an equal. I'm good with languages and speak the Lacota Sioux language as well or better than most of them." He winced at a thought. "Six brothers," he said aloud. "Do you believe it? Six? Hard to believe they were all that bad a shot. Maybe they were trying to miss." He laughed. "Story of my life!"

The old woman pinched her mouth into a disapproving expression.

Mitchell produced a bottle of Jack Daniels whiskey and offered a sip to the fellow traveler. The grandmotherly, hawkish woman, who Mitchell hadn't noticed when he sat down made a disgusted sound.

The exhausted Mitchell looked at her light grey over-robe covered with hand-embroidered symbols that Mitchell did not recognize.

A leftover flower child, Mitchell thought with a wry smile. *Not unlike myself.*

"No thank you, young man," she said in a brittle tone. "I can do without spirits as can you. You look more like you could use some sleep." The train chose that moment to suddenly lurch and Mitchell spilled whiskey all down his denim shirt.

T.K. ignored the spill, shrugged his shoulders and smiled. "Sleep and I just don't get along, ma'am, but sometimes this helps."

Mitchell slumped against his seat studying his reflection in the train window. He realized that he was not so much tired from the hours of relentless pursuit through the worst terrain on the Black Hills Indian reservation, as from the annoying frequency with which siblings, spouses and outraged parents were doing that sort of thing to him of late. "I'm getting too old for this sort of nonsense," he said, taking a drink. "Though, I don't know what nonsense to replace it with."

At forty-three, Teel Kantos Mitchell had a handsome face, weathered by many nights on park benches across the country; his once brown hair was streaked with flecks of grey, as was his neatly trimmed beard. He wore a gold hoop through the lobe of his left ear. In a happier age he would have been called a hippie. Now the word 'bum' came first to his mind when he saw his own image.

"Have you no more respect for your family than to dress and live like that?" the old woman across from him asked in a quiet but commanding tone that put Mitchell in mind of a Sunday school teacher that had kicked him out of bible class when he was nine.

"I'm afraid I've got nobody but me, lady."

"No mother; father?" she asked.

"Dead," he said quietly, aware of his own voice in the silence of the near empty passenger car. Outside the clacking of the wheels on the tracks was hypnotic. "Got a no-good younger brother floating around somewhere; and a sponge of an ex-wife in New York—if you can call them family. I like to call them history. Ancient history. All I got in this world and the next is sitting in this backpack, ma'am. Never had any other home than this; ain't felt at home anywhere since my folks died. Always just lookin' over the next hill for my place in the world," he concluded. He took a deep swig from the bottle then smacked his lips.

"Don't you have any respect for yourself? Surely you feel responsibility to family heritage for some..."

"'Scuse my rudeness, Ma'am, but you got no right to lecture me on anything. So hows about you just let me see if I've had enough of this 'medicine' to sleep so I can dream of Lacota princesses and nearsighted brothers, okay? It hasn't been one of my best days; I'm gonna miss Whitefawn." To cut off further conversation he hunkered down on the seat next to his backpack and closed his eyes, hoping he was buzzed enough to sleep.

He never had the chance to more than close his eyes as the train suddenly lurched to a stop. T.K. was thrown to the floor with his pack landing on top of him.

"What the hell?" he clichéd, as did half the train car of passengers sprawled in similar positions. He righted himself and noticed that the old woman was not anywhere in sight. *Odd old duck,* he thought.

"Hey, conductor," somebody else in the car yelled. "What's going on?"

The middle-aged conductor struggled down the aisle, fighting for his own dignity after being dumped on the carpet. "I'll let you folks know as soon as I know for sure," he called out. "But it feels like somebody pulled the emergency cord." He hurried out of the car heading toward the engine.

Mitchell had barely enough time (and consciousness) to notice that the train had stopped in a tunnel before the conductor came swiftly back into the car muttering curses.

"What's wrong?" someone up front yelled.

"Some crazy Indians have stopped the train," the conductor said in an annoyed tone. "Claim there's a thief on board and they have jurisdiction since the crime happened on their reservation."

Oh Crap and crumbs on toast! Mitchell thought, *They just don't give up and they're more inventive than I gave them credit for. They came up with a legal reason to beat me senseless.*

He quietly gathered up his pack and an intricately carved walking stick, doing his best to be invisible while he limped to the rear door of the train car. *I really hate having to do this all the time,* he thought.

Mitchell could hear a commotion toward the front of the train when he jumped clumsily down to the gravel track bed. That decided him to head back along the cars at a trot.

The tunnel was inky black and warmer than one would expect from September. So warm, in fact, that he ran into clouds of steam.

Freaky, he thought, *this is too strange a cloud of steam for condensation. And the train is supposed to be a diesel train.*

A sudden hiss from an air brake made him half turn his head toward the sound. That meant he had no chance to see the hole he stepped into and caught his foot.

T.K. Mitchell pitched forward with the velocity of his run and with his arms flung out behind him. He had the final thought, *You were only worth this, Whitefawn, honey, if they just beat me into a coma and don't actually kill me.*

And then his head hit the concrete wall of the tunnel.

WHITE LIGHT!

Sudden and intense like a million flashbulbs popping at once, the light kept flashing but with no sound at all. T.K. felt as if he had been thrown into a tub of gelatin, as if the world had gone cotton candy and he was in a funhouse. He was still falling forward but his tumble forward slowed.

Man, this is the weirdest concussion dream.

A female voice called his attention left and he found he could turn his head at normal speed.

"Teel," a translucent figure, attired in a long grey robe said. She stood in a swirling cloud of yellow vapor so that she seemed a ghostly figure. It was the old woman from the train but somehow different. "I am Meegana Rakdon." The woman spoke as if he should know the name.

"Glad to meet you again," he said as politely as possible from his forty-five-degree angle. He thought, *Class A-One hallucination, T.K. old bean, keep up the good work.*

"I have intermittently followed the progress of your life and that of your brother with both keen interest and deep disgust, Teel Kantos," the old woman called Meegana said, "though, regrettably, I must say I can currently find no trace of your brother."

"V.J. and I haven't spoken for eight years, lady," T.K. said, "Last time I told him to get lost, he took my advice to heart."

"Enough, Meegana," a rougher voice to Mitchell's right said. "We need to see proof!"

"Patience, General Thorvanus," Meegana said. "The boy is apparently a bit bewildered."

"Naw, lady," T.K. said. "I'm like this all the time."

"—And must be made to understand the importance of the circumstances," the grey crone continued as if T.K. had not spoken.

"Teel Kantos, you have been told, no doubt, by your mother that she was a refugee," Meegana began, "but she undoubtedly did not tell you a refugee from where or why she had to flee."

T.K. enjoyed the sensation of floating slowly downward, only vaguely aware of the woman speaking so gave no reply.

"Sphona, your mother, was a princess of the Royal House of Mephistal on the island of Mephan to the west of the twin continents on the world of Altiva."

T.K. mouthed the word "Right," but did not vocalize it.

"Your mother was the daughter of Emperor Kantos, the world's most powerful ruler," Meegana continued. "And as such was promised to wed the wizard Roosuf, a first cousin. He was a warp wizard of considerable craft and temporal power. Though this alliance would strengthen the empire, Sphona was against it for... personal reasons."

"Personal, ha!" A new male voice chimed in with a hearty laugh. "Roosuf is a gross and barbarous monster. Her personal reason was taste, my dear."

T.K. listened to the exchange from his increasingly steep incline with only casual interest. The old woman spoke to the phantom male voice. "Respectfully you must be quiet, Duke Havros, time is short." Then she addressed T.K. again.

"The young princess compounded her father's wrath at her refusal to marry the wizard with the one disease royalty should never contract— love of commoner. When she discovered she was with child by this court artisan, she was terrified. She sought the help to escape with the father of one who cared for her greatly, her court warp wizard. The court wizard spirited the two lovers to another plane, that which you call Earth, where they would be safe from pursuit." The old woman paused for breath and to let her words sink in. "I was that court wizard."

From his seventy-degree inclination T.K. considered what the old woman had said and then sagely asked, "What's this got to do with me?" he said as he continued to slowly fall.

Meegana all but sputtered with frustration.

"He is an idiot!" Thorvanus cursed.

"The Wizard Roosuf inherited the throne," the woman continued with an edge of anger in her tone. "—when the young Emperor Meartus, brother to Sphona, fell victim to a mysterious ailment and died after only two years reign. We are sure it was warpcraft!"

The voice of the one called Duke Havros said, "But craft could not be proved and so Roosuf assumed the throne and has ruled with a merciless hand for three oppressive years."

"Sorry, but I'm not up on political science," T.K. asked innocently. "How does this connect to me exactly?"

"You are the key to Roosuf's downfall, for you are the rightful ruler of Mephistal and thus he must step down to you." Meegana said.

"If he has the mark," Thorvanus insisted. "We must have proof he has the mark."

"What mark?" The eighty-one degree suspended and very confused T.K. asked.

"The birthmark of the line of Kantos. All members of the line have such a mark on their arm!"

"Oh, that." T.K. raised his left arm above his head, delighting in the liquid slow movement. Once raised, he indicated the inside of the left bicep, where one of the many rents in his denim shirt revealed a scarlet birthmark in the shape of three crescents. "I've always had that," T.K. said, "So do Mom and V.J."

"And so has every member of the Royal House since—" The old woman stopped talking abruptly. Then T.K. heard a distant pounding in the phantom space where the old woman and the others were.

"The wizard has detected my warpcraft," Meegana said. "I cannot complete the process here."

"He must be brought through," another voice that T.K. could not identify said.

"Listen, Teel Kantos," the old woman said, "I must bring you into our world far from your goal of Mephistal, but I will find you within two tenday. It is the only location with a warp open that I know the wizard can not find. Until that time I can come to you, be the utmost cautious." The spectral shapes in front of T.K. began to blur. "An Emperor uncrowned had best always be cautious."

"But I don't want to be no damn—" Suddenly his nose touched earth.
WHITE LIGHT!

Chapter Two

"A good time to keep your mouth shut is when you're in deep water."
T. K. Mitchell

T.K. Mitchell hit the ground hard and lay breathing in short gasps, the weight of the backpack that held the entirety of his life's legacy driving most of the air out of him. He lay with his eyes closed, feeling the damp, cool earth pressed against his right cheek.

That was the strangest bullet hit I've ever taken, he decided. *I wonder where I'm wounded, must'a hit me in the head for this kind of reaction.* He didn't move for a while, searching all his body for the pain or numbness that should be there. *I must still be in shock,* he thought when he felt no fresh pain. He remained motionless, afraid to find out just where the irate Indian had shot him.

Eventually, with great trepidation, he opened his eyes.

The only thing he could see was a clump of reddish weeds a few feet away, which impressed him in one respect; it was broad daylight!

I must have been hit bad, maybe in the head and they left me for dead! He waited a long moment before hauling himself up on his elbows.

It was then he heard the sound that marked a major turning point in his life. It sounded like "Zeth mey zo?" but in a deep, whispered voice. T.K. looked up at the source of the voice and made a sound like "oh!"

Seated astride a great black horse (it looked more like a horse than anything else, though the steed's antlers, beak and red mane marked it as most definitely not a horse) was a man. He looked several hard years older than T.K. with a rugged face that had been handsome in youth. His hair and goatee were short cropped and jet black and he was smiling.

This latter fact was good because he was also armed with a disturbing array of weapons: a saber with a hand guard in the shape of a skull at his left hip, two short poniard-like weapons at his right hip, a back-sheathed sword of the two-handed variety under a cover and four serpentine-shaped throwing knives tucked into a broad sash around his waist.

T.K. smiled back.

The rider wore a rough sewn sleeveless leather shirt and trunks with a throat-protecting cowl piece hanging open off his left shoulder. He wore knee-high leather puttees and what appeared to be chaps strapped on in order to protect the insides of his thighs from his mount's sides while riding.

The stranger tried again. "Zeth mew eth mey zo?" he asked, his voice a harsh whisper. Still he smiled, so T.K. did not perceive an immediate threat so smiled a bit broader himself.

Mitchell studied the man further and found the reason for the whisper: there was an ugly scar almost from ear to ear on the stranger's throat. The scar was long healed and from the look of it had been poorly sutured. The other striking feature was a peculiar pattern of scar tissue in the center of the man's chest that appeared to be some sort of brand in the shape of three interlocked diamonds.

T.K. pushed himself to his knees and then stood up, startled that, after patting himself down, he found no wounds. The rider watched T.K.'s self-appraisal with a stoic expression. When T. K. was done, he looked around. For the first time, he realized things had changed.

The train tunnel and the mountains were gone.

Instead, he now stood on a flat plain by a small lake surrounded by rolling, gentle hills stretched out as far as the eye could see. The daylight was oddly different than a Dakota afternoon but he could not figure out what the difference was. It took him a moment to realize why: everything had two shadows. One shadow was tinted pink and one tinted blue which gave everything a theatrical quality.

He gasped when he saw that the sun was now small, pink, and not alone! A second orb, larger and blue, sat neatly, not far above the horizon.

The rider cleared his throat to get T.K.'s attention, and then by sign language made T.K. understand he wanted him to put on the small, strangely carved crystal ring that he held out.

I hope this doesn't mean we're engaged, T.K. thought as he slipped it on. There was a sudden tingle in his head and a buzzing in his ears but it quickly passed.

"Can you understand me now, sirrah?" the rider asked in his hoarse whisper.

"Sure, but what I..." T.K. started and then froze. He did. He did understand the man's words. Somehow, he knew it was not because the man had suddenly switched to speaking English! This sure as hell isn't Kansas, T.K. thought. Then he managed an eloquent, "How?"

"All questions in their own rhythm, sirrah, but answer me this first: are you a cannibal?"

T.K. stared at the man and Spockly arched an eyebrow. "What?"

"An eater of sentient flesh?" The man's manner was so straightforward and sincere that T.K. caught himself examining his memory for personal violations in line with the stranger's question. He shook his head.

"Hell no, never touch the stuff," T.K. said emphatically. "Clogs the arteries and fills nervous system with toxins."

"Good," the stranger said as if from personal experience. "I can't abide cannibals."

"I agree," T.K. agreed wholeheartedly. "They're a bore at parties."

The strangely attired man slid from the saddle of his mount without so much as a clink from his frightening array of cutlery and walked back to one of the pack 'horses'—there were three that T.K. had not noticed before. He started to hunt through one of the packs and finally pulled out the blanket he was looking for. He also took out a length of rope and moved to one of the beasts that was burdened with only a small pack, which he proceeded to remove.

"I assume you are curious about where you are," the stranger said, "and how you got here." He cut a length of rope, threw a blanket over the animal's bare back, and lashed it on with the rope.

"The thought had crossed my mind."

The stranger laughed a strange, whispered laugh.

"By the Rhythem, my manners seem to have fled me." He turned and made an elaborate bow. "My name is The Reverend Lord Erique, The Shoutte of Shoutte. I am, as you see, a Priest of the Kova."

This has got to be a drug-induced fantasy, T.K. thought, *and I've got to find out who prescribed this drug and where he got it.* "Pleased to meet you, if somewhat puzzled," T.K. said lightly with his own improvised bow.

He removed his torn denim shirt and stored its remains in his backpack. From the pack he removed and then donned a buckskin vest with intricate beadwork in red, green, and blue with a stylized butterfly, a Lakota symbol for eternal life and memory. It had been a present Whitefawn had given him. He smiled, thinking of the lovely Lacota woman one last time before consigning her to his mental hall of might-have-been loves.

"My name's T.K. Mitchell," he said aloud. "Glad to meet you."

"Tee-Kay? Strange name." The stranger laughed a strange, whispered laugh. His expression said that laughing was something that came easily to him.

Lord Shoutte produced a small parchment scroll from a belt pouch and unfurled it to reveal a carefully drawn map. It showed three vaguely crescent-shaped islands with a variety of unreadable symbols and scrawling.

"By the Rhythem, let me tell you where you are." He pointed first to the map and then spread his hands in an expansive gesture to take in the plain around them. "This is the high road to Tolan, capital of Cosen. As you see, we are on the north continent of the world called Altiva."

He cut a length of rope, threw a blanket over the animal's bare back, and lashed it on with the rope.

"Altiva? But how… here?" He held up the ring and looked questioningly at Lord Shoutte. "This?"

"The linguaring is a wizard charm. Ask me not how it works, I am but a simple priest." Lord Shoutte shrugged. "The Warp Wizards do many things better left unquestioned." He said the last of it as if he were quoting a rote saying, not as if he believed it.

T.K. leaned against his walking stick and, with a measure of disgust, said, "Come on, uh...Lord Shoutte, straight! How did I get here?" Even as he asked it, the momentary fantasy of the old woman from the train and a vague memory of shadowy figures at the edge of his consciousness— it seemed important, but like a dream once wakened he could not quite remember what that memory was. *Can you have an acid trip within an acid trip?* he wondered.

"The warps, of course," Lord Shoutte whispered indignantly. "I heard a wizard once speak about them. He said that there was a civilization that used the warp portals as you or I would use a common door. Then something happened. The Rhythem was fulfilled and the civilization was gone. But the warps remained." He scratched his chin reflexively. "Now people and things are always dropping through one warp or another."

T.K. just stared at the man and nodded, more in shock than understanding. "Yeah, sure."

Lord Shoutte walked back to his own mount and placed a foot in the ornate stirrup. "Well, sirrah, hop aboard." He stepped up into his own saddle and motioned to the blanketed back of the pack animal. His expression changed to concern when, as he watched, T.K. looked around as if some unseen third party were the 'sirrah' in question.

"Hop aboard?" T.K. said.

"I believe I said that already." Lord Shoutte leaned forward and evidenced considerable annoyance. His whispered voice took on an edge. "You do want to find a warp wizard to help you find a way back to your own world? Most warp orphans make that a priority when they arrive."

"Off to see the wizard, huh? I believe it is the thing to do under the circumstances."

"You can ride, can you not?" Lord Shoutte asked.

T.K. jumped astride the former pack animal's back. "Bareback, on my head, or blind drunk," he said. "Lead on, Macduff!"

Chapter Three

"Life is a Joke; you either get the punch line or you are the punch line."
One-legged orderly in a V.A. hospital.

The two new companions rode off at a leisurely pace, but every once in a while the earthman found himself looking up at the sky, as if he expected a house to drop on him.

The world that Reverend Lord Shoutte called Altiva (or at least the part that T.K. saw on the first day's ride) reminded the reluctant visitor of Ireland, but it was an acid trip Ireland of gently rolling hills that seemed in constant motion because of the twin shadows the two suns cast as the different-sized orbs moved across the sky at different rates.

The double shadow gave T.K. the most trouble in judging distance and relative size. He found himself doing a mental double take on several occasions when something seemed to have moved that hadn't. *Unless large boulders on Altiva shiver.*

Lord Shoutte proved an amiable traveling companion, full of anecdotes, bawdy jokes, and interesting trivia about Altiva—all of which had value to T.K.

The earthman, for his part, entertained Lord Shoutte with his own bawdy jokes and some travel stories that had been bizarre even back on good old Terra Firma.

At some point Lord Shoutte noticed the tattoo of the Marine Corps emblem on T.K.'s left arm and remarked, "I see you have a skill mark."

"A skill mark?" T.K. said as he idly studied the stone ruins of a building that had come into view over the next hill. They were red and green stone and overgrown with vines and looked to be of considerable age.

"Has anyone ever told you that you have an annoying tendency of repeating what has been said to you, sir?" Lord Shoutte whispered.

The dark-haired warrior indicated the design branded onto the center of his chest. T.K. noted that the triple diamond branding seemed to be made at three different times; each long after the previous had healed.

"These proclaim me as a full priest of the Kova," Lord Shoutte said. "Priestsinger, healer, and warrior. Each brand earned at the end of a three-year study period in the subject. What does your skill mark mean?" When he pointed to T.K.'s tattoo the earthman laughed so hard he almost choked.

"It means that once I was mean, tough, and too stupid not to volunteer,"

T.K. said and then added sagely, "I somehow lived to be older and wiser; still no idea how that happened." Lord Shoutte looked very puzzled, as if he were going to say something but he thought better of it. He reined up his mount next to the first of the ruins.

"Let us tether the vorns here," he rasped, "and make camp. The wind blows cold at night hereabouts. These half-fallen walls will serve us well. Finally, this old Ashun temple is useful for something."

T.K. climbed down off his mount, stretched and massaged his sore behind. "Been a while since I did any riding worth counting. These things ain't much different than mustangs."

The scared priest gave a short, pleasant laugh. "These are unusually calm for vorns, who do tend to be bad tempered with anyone but me; you did well."

"You see to the beasties, then," T. K. said acknowledging the compliment. "I'll gather enough firewood to last the night." Mitchell handed his reins to Lord Shoutte and walked off in the direction of several low walls that appeared to have once encased an orchard or garden of an ancient estate. The manor house of the ruined dwelling was a shell of crumbling blue and green stone beyond the orchard, away from what Shoutte had called a temple.

Blue leaved trees marched across the hillside in carefully staggered rows that had clearly been planned by design. Firewood was plentiful at the foot of the trees and he marveled at the comfort of the familiar ritual of gathering it for a campfire.

Holy spit, T.K. thought, *it just doesn't seem real. Last night I was with a sweet Sioux princess while we hid out from her brothers and now...* He laughed to himself. *Well, his legs aren't as nice as hers, but at least he's nobility too.*

The former Marine looked up at the darkening sky and tried to imagine what constellations might be out there if indeed he was on a different world and not in his own head or a coma. After a few moments gave up when he seemed to hear that spectral woman from his 'dream' in the tunnel, *"An Emperor uncrowned had best always be cautious."*

"But I don't want to be no damn Emperor," T.K. said aloud, with his own voice startling him. He looked around embarrassed. "Oh, man," he whispered to himself, "I am having flashbacks to places I haven't been. What the hell kind of dream is that?"

He shook himself to banish off the vision and carried his third armload of wood back to camp where he stacked some of it into a neat pile beneath a wide arch. Lord Shoutte had set down their gear beneath the arch and gathered some dried grass for kindling. T.K., out of habit, removed a flint kit from his pack and began trying to spark a fire in the kindling.

Lord Shoutte, who was feeding the animals in a makeshift corral of rubble nearby, laughed. "No need for that, Tee-Kay." Lord Shoutte finished with the animals and walked over to watch T.K.'s progress with interest.

"I ran out of matches," T.K. explained. Lord Shoutte looked puzzled so the earthman added, "to start the fire."

"You've no need of firebrands. I have Rhythemwand." He reached behind him and tapped the agate handle of the sword he had uncovered and which was slung across his back. The handle was an intricately carved feathered dragon, which curved around a central grip serving as knuckle guard, its open mouth gripping a blood-red pommel stone.

Lord Shoutte drew the sword and held it aloft, clearing the sheath with practiced elegance. The blade looked as if it had been carved out of translucent crystal, holding the last rays of the setting second sun and throwing back a small rainbow. It glowed as if from within—as if it had its own living brilliance.

Lord Shoutte brought the weapon down in a shallow arc that struck a rock near the kindling with a calculated glancing blow. Sparks leapt from the rock and the kindling was soon smoldering.

T.K. had jumped as the sword arced then controlled himself and fixed haunted eyes on the sword. It took great effort but he reluctantly stayed kneeling close to the wood, feeding the kindling and blowing on it till he had nursed the fire into full life.

Lord Shoutte sheathed the sword with almost melancholy reluctance, sliding the crystal blade into place on his back with casual perfection of motion that bespoke uncounted hours of practice.

"Neat trick," T.K. whispered as he continued to feed branches into the fire keeping his eyes focused on the flames.

"No trick, not Rhythemwand," Lord Shoutte said with a touch of pain in his whispered reply. "It was grown by a crystalsmith in my own blood to bond it to me. It will shatter when I die and I will die should it ever shatter. They say only another crystal blade can do it harm."

The priest stood proudly, his fingers caressing the dragon handle that seemed imbued with life in the flickering light of the fire. "Some say that a crystal blade molds itself to the purpose of the user at bonding, so if the user is evil it will be a cursed sword; if he serves a just cause only the just may hold it." He sighed with his gaze inward to his own remembered adventures, a full range of emotions playing across his features. "Rhythemwand," he said with finality about the sword. "My soul."

T.K. pointed to the saber on Lord Shoutte's belt. "What do you call that one?" he asked.

Lord Shoutte looked at him as if he were a bit simple. "Why, it is just a sword."

T.K. caught implication of the tone. He grabbed his walking stick and rose. "Come on, Fred," he mumbled to the stick, "let's go take a piss."

Lord Shoutte watched him leave with a puzzled expression.

✦✦✦

Dinner for the two new acquaintances consisted of a stew of meat and vegetables, none of which T.K. could identify, a fact that that only slightly discomforted him yet which went down with ease. It was followed by a grain that was heated in oil and popped like corn which had a sweet taste and finished the meal on a high note.

"Whatever that grain was," T.K. said as he sat back against a boulder and picked his teeth with a twig, "it was very good."

He leaned forward and gathered the wooden plates to scrape them down with some of the sandy soil. "I'll do the dishes, you cooked." The earthman rose and took the bowls and plates to a small bubbling spring among the ruins where he then washed them off with the water.

Lord Shoutte took feedbags to the mounts then returned to the campfire from the animals, determinedly chewing a piece of licorice that T.K. had given him.

"I have to thank you again for the hospitality, Lord Shoutte," T.K. said when he was done with the plates.

"It is both a pleasure and a duty," Lord Shoutte said. "Pity though you have no dice. I crave a game and I lost my dice in the last town after an argument with some who were violently anti-Kovar." He contentedly chewed off another hunk of the licorice. "Hmm. I like this Lick-or-ish."

"That was the last of a batch I picked up in Bismarck," T.K. said with a smile, remembering the circumstances of his trip to the city. "Not a stick left."

"Pity. It would have made the rhythm of days more enjoyable. To the Rhythem!" he exclaimed. Then he reached into a saddlebag and pulled out a small package wrapped in oilcloth. He unwrapped it to reveal a green gelatinous cake, which he tossed to T.K. "I do have this tranya to satisfy my sweet tooth. Cut yourself a piece. And a small piece for me."

"I'll pass," T.K. said, his tone suddenly over-friendly. "The law of averages is stacked against three alien dishes agreeing with my stomach in one night."

Lord Shoutte used one of his throwing daggers to cut off a chunk of the green cake then returned the tranya to its wrapping.

"I thought you wouldn't," Lord Shoutte said in his hoarse whisper. "I saw that you made no use of the dinner knife either." He bit off a healthy chunk of the tranya and chewed it slowly, his eyes never leaving T.K.'s. The Earthman returned the stare with gentle animosity.

"I just don't like things with blades," T.K. said.

Lord Shoutte let out a deep breath. "You'll not do well on this world with a dislike of that nature, Tee-Kay. This is a sword's world." As if the statement needed reinforcing, Lord Shoutte touched the hilt of the saber lying beside him.

T.K.'s glance at the weapon held an emotion closer to disgust than fear.

"I've made do in some pretty tough places without resorting to knives," T.K. said with quiet bravado.

Lord Shoutte's reply, couched in his hoarse whisper, was a chilling one. "Altiva is not a tough place, my new friend, it is a deadly one." He spoke matter-of-factly and touched the long scar at his throat. "My people, the Kovar, are the most tolerant, perhaps the most peaceful, loving people on this world, yet we are always armed. We have to be; that very tolerance is considered weakness by some."

T.K.'s answer betrayed the fact that he was becoming annoyed. "I'm not defenseless." He forced a laugh when he realized how brash he sounded. "Not by a long shot, pal. Hell, you're a priest, right? So how come you're preaching killing? Barry Fitzgerald used to preach love and all that."

Lord Shoutte stopped in mid-chew of the tranya and drew himself up to full-seated height. "I preach the Kova, sirrah, the Supreme Principle, that of Change Eternal." He swallowed the last of his snack. "It is the only constant in the universe, the one above all others and to which even all deities are subject. Life to death, day to night, sick to well." All anger was gone from his voice now he had an even smile like the devout man he was, imparting truth.

"The Kova, the center of my life, teaches me to accept any and all change that comes in my way, and work to keep peace and do good." He continued with a smile, "I preach change, but if some fool wishes to try and harm me or an innocent against the Rhythem of the Universe, I just help his

...NOW HE HAD AN EVEN SMILE...

transition to the next plane."

T.K. smiled back. "I heard a Hell's Angel give a speech like that in Phoenix. He decided to try to beat me to a pulp right afterward." He threw a few more branches on the fire, and began laying out his bedroll.

"Was he successful?" Lord Shoutte asked.

"Actually," T.K. stripped off his vest, "Yeah. He beat the living hell out of me. But, on reflection, considering what I told him about his ancestors, I probably deserved it." Lord Shoutte stared at him for a moment and then began to laugh, the sound made strange by his inability to talk above a whisper. T.K. took a moment to realize what he had said, and joined in.

"Well, chum," T.K. said when the moment had passed, "I'm exhausted. It's been a long time since I've taken a trip to another world." He unlaced his hiking boots and settled down.

"Sleep with the Rhythem, Tee-Kay. And, again, welcome to Altiva." The priest moved to the other side of the fire and stretched out his bedroll near his saddle. T.K. lay back staring up at the strange sky and listened to the priest settle in until he begin breathing rhythmically.

T.K. was awake for a long time, taking in the unfamiliar yet oddly calming night sounds of this new world called Altiva. Dual moons filled the expanse above and lit the countryside around the ruined buildings as brightly as a summer twilight or a harvest moon back on earth.

My God, he thought, *this is so real yet so freakin' bizarre.* Lord Shoutte was real and the earth (or was it Altiva?) beneath him was real enough, particularly the stones beneath his bedroll. It was like the world had taken a right turn at reality somewhere—starting with that phantom woman, Meegana.

'Emperor,' Meegana *said.* He grinned. *And me busted back to E 2 three separate times!*

T.K. Mitchell thought of his mother.

He saw her in his mind's eye, bringing a hot lunch down the hill from the house to the shed where his father chipped and shaped heaps of stone into grave monuments. She brought down his lunch so he wouldn't track dust into her immaculate house and to share his work with him for a little while. The two would laugh and joke and smile for a bit all the way to the end.

So strong, so proud, so gentle a woman. It was easy enough to imagine her as the daughter of an emperor. And so sad a woman it was believable she had given it up. As a ten-year-old boy he heard her one night seated at the kitchen table crying. He was about to rush to comfort her when his father's calloused, gentle hand stopped him.

"Why is mother crying?" the young T.K. had asked.

"Your mother likes to go home in her memory now and again, son," his father said quietly, "because it is the only way she can go home." His father was a great bear of a man who was a monument to strength himself, yet at that moment the boy could see the anguish in him, the utter helplessness that suffused his entire being.

I think I see now, Dad, T.K. thought. *You loved her so much, yet there was one thing you couldn't give her—a simple trip home.*

He thought about the story of his parents that Meegana had told him. He searched his childhood memories for facts that would verify the story. Could all the frequent moves when he was young, the suspicion of strangers that his parents drilled into him and the attitude of self-reliance his father had instilled in both he and his brother V.J. been because they were on the run from an empire on another world? It all seemed so absurd and yet considering the thousand little questions he had all his life, with the template of that fear of pursuit superimposed over a million tiny actions that otherwise would have no connection, a pattern emerged. Suddenly all the questions were answered with one simple fact; that Meegana's story was true.

In the most sensible of ways, the nonsensical made perfect sense.

The feeling of being pursued faded by the time T.K. had reached his teens and his folks had felt safe enough to settle down and buy a house.

I guess you two had it a lot tougher than I could have imagined, he thought to his parents. *Thanks.*

He felt a chill and pulled a thermal undershirt from his pack and donned it before settling down to try to sleep again.

The mounts snorted and kicked in the improvised corral and Lord Shoutte rose from near the fire to go check on them. T.K. watched him go with a stray thought about what sort of nocturnal creatures roamed on Altiva, but he didn't *really* want to know.

You were always so evasive about our family background, Mom, T.K. thought, *but it seems just about right that you were a fairy tale princess.*

His parents had died of pneumonia a week apart when he was twenty. Right up until the end they had been as affectionate as newlyweds. T.K. pulled his sleeping bag tighter around him against a sudden gust of wind. He rolled over and ignored the distant cry of a night bird.

He realized he was crying and wiped the tears away feeling a little silly. *I thought I was done with crying in my life. But I've been wrong so often before—why not now?*

His final thought before sleep claimed him had become almost a litany to him. *God, let me have just one night without dreams. Just one night without the nightmare.*

+++

From somewhere beyond the mounts the shrill cry of the ko-ta bird sounded a second time and the burly man known only to his men as Axe knew his followers were in place at last.

The camp where their prey was sleeping was now surrounded. The first of the scouts had trailed the priest and the warp orphan since late afternoon, but the rest had not arrived until only an hour ago.

Axe, crouched in the shadows of a large boulder, had been with the scout team and had stayed behind to keep an eye on the outworlder. The Wizard Emperor had instructed the group to kill the warp orphan with full dispatch. Axe did not think that would be any problem, the priest might be difficult, though; it was not wise to face a skill-marked Kovar without the odds being in one's favor. The priest was the reason Axe had sent for reinforcements and waited.

The priest's mounts had caught scent of the arriving band but no one had been seen. Axe had deployed his men around the camp after making them leave their mounts far enough away so that changes in the wind would not carry either scent or sound to alert the skill-marked one. Nothing would go wrong with this ambush; the cost of reporting failure to Axe's employer had been made all too clear.

Axe watched the priest return to his bedroll and was a little surprised when the careless cleric doused the bright fire.

Stupid holy man, Axe thought when his eyes had readjusted to the dark so he could see the shape of the priest's bedroll. *So confident that you don't care that there might be bandits about?* He chuckled viciously at his own joke.

The priest had rolled himself into his bedroll with his back to Axe, a bundle of bedding ready for the slaughter. The outworlder, across the cleric on the other side of the smothered fire, was already snoring loudly.

"Stupid priest," Axe whispered. He spit and rose, grasping the long-handled war axe from which he took his name. He leaned his head back to cry "Kooo-ta!" a third time to call his men in for the attack.

A circle of steel detached itself from the shadows as fifteen shapes moved forward on the call to arms.

Let the others deal with the priest, Zomar damn him, Axe thought. *It will be my axe that takes the warp orphan's head as a prize for Lord Gavilon—in one clean stroke.* He smiled with anticipation and moved forward.

Chapter Four

"Beauty be only skin deep, But ugliness goes to da' bone."
The Kingfish

The Younger Brother cast oblique rays through the morning mists, highlighting the soaring spires and squat waterfront warehouses of Mephan City. It was not quite full dawn, for the larger sun, the Elder Brother, would not rise for a quarter-hour.

Watching from the windowed turret of the palace, Roosuf, the Wizard Emperor of the Mephistal Empire, cursed the dawn. "Burn in the Ephindal Pits, Meegana," Roosuf whispered to himself. "You've opposed me at every turn, fought my policies in the Council of Barons, schemed against me in secret but I could never act as I wished—" He threw the words out over the city as if the last shadows of the night would carry his envenomed words to the woman wizard's ears. "Now your use of warpcraft in defiance of my edict gives me a free hand to destroy you!"

Roosuf was a big man with a massive bald head that seemed to join his body sans neck. His broad-shouldered physique, barrel chest and extended gut would have seemed more in character for a tavern keeper were it not for the grace with which his massive hands moved. This grace told of countless arcane patterns invoked by the delicate flourish of a finger. They and his very presence evoked an aura of power and spoke of tremendous energy in his every move.

"Your Majesty." A voice of like that of the grave disturbed the Wizard Emperor's thoughts.

Roosuf turned to face his chief vassal, Gavilon of Belisle, the Lord High Executioner.

The vassal stood as tall and gaunt as death and was clad in a long, midnight black mail coat and horned battle helm whose vorn's horns crest had become the symbol for terror among the people of the realm.

The executioner removed the helm to reveal a face that never saw the suns, made whiter by bloodless lips and soulless eyes that reflected less light than his dark armor. He waited, motionless until his lord spoke.

"You have news for me of Thorvanus?" Roosuf said, "Good news?"

"The General still proves…ah…difficult," Gavilon said. His voice was all but toneless, like an echo in a tomb.

The Wizard Emperor grunted with displeasure.

"He is the only one of those captured who remains alive, Master." Gavilon stood statue still before Roosuf. His posture did not betray the fear of his Emperor that any other in the realm had but few doubted he felt it, if he felt anything.

"Then why are you here?" The Royal's voice cut like a blade.

"He may not live much longer, Your Majesty. He is not a young man and I have been—thorough."

Roosuf considered for a moment and with a grace that belied his size, swept past Lord Gavilon and out of the room.

His vassal followed death's shadow.

+++

General Thorvanus could hear Death's whisper, "The heir, Thorvanus, tell me of the heir."

The General was confused. The pain was beyond pain. Gavilon had stripped the skin from most of his body and gouged out the old man's eyes. His nose was a pulpy mess and his fingers were all broken. There was no pain anymore, no attachment to his body at all. He floated in a void from which he heard Death's whisper speak to him. It was like a comforting embrace to know he was not alone in the void.

"Where is the heir, Thorvanus? You must tell me so I can protect him. I will keep him safe from those who wish to harm him. Then the revolution can proceed. That is what you want, is it not? Tell me!"

It was so difficult for the tortured man to concentrate, but the general forced himself. *The* heir. Protect the heir.

"Too dangerous to leave the heir on the Earth plane," the General whispered, "That monster Roosuf was too close to discovering where he was hiding."

"Then where is the heir?" the comforting voice floated all around Thorvanus, "Tell me where he is. I must know! I can protect him. You want that, do you not? To protect him?"

"Cosen," Thorvanus murmured. "It is far enough away that Roosuf will not find him there for a time. Time. We need time…" The pain grew greater and the voice faded.

The void became all-encompassing to the tortured man with the mercy of fading consciousness.

+++

The Wizard Emperor turned away from the near dead man suspended from the dungeon wall. "Cosen," he whispered with venom in his tone, "Hmm! I must consult the charts for that area." He stared into space for a moment his gaze focused inward then abruptly turned to his subordinate.

"Lord Gavilon, I will join you in the south courtyard in one hour after I have studied the warp portal charts. Be prepared for a hard ride."

+++

It was just a little less than an hour later that Lord Gavilon was in the courtyard of the palace. He was mounted on a black war charger in full battle armor, provisions for a week's hard ride lashed behind him as waited for his master.

The executioner sat astride the war vorn unmoving, looking like a monument to horror and death. He looked neither left nor right nor made any sound, empty for half an hour, waiting for his master Roosuf's command. No spark of life glowed in his pitch-black eyes until they caught sight of the Wizard Emperor passing the guard at the courtyard entrance.

"I have consulted the warp charts," Roosuf proclaimed, "and they inform me that there is but one portal on the east face of the northern continent that could have been open when that hag brought the heir through." He stepped up to beside the mounted vassal and his face split into a grin. "The bitch has outsmarted herself with this move. The council has no power to stay my hand in that country and there will be no one to report his ultimate fate, eh?"

"None, my Lord," Gavilon said in a flat voice. Roosuf looked at him oddly.

"My faithful Gavilon, by whom of all my subjects I am asked least."

"I ask only to serve, master; my soul is yours."

"Yes," the Emperor said lightly, "I know." He reached into the folds of his elegant robes and produced a small cage in which a scrawny creature with leathery wings watched the men sullenly with red eyes.

"The only available portal I can send you through today will place you almost a week's ride from where the heir arrived on Altiva. Release this messenger with this amulet attached when you have crossed through the portal." He produced a serpent pendant on a chain. "My agents closer to his entry point have already begun the search. This messenger will be your link with them, when they receive this they will know you have come in my name." Gavilon took both the offered objects.

"Bring back his head, Gavilon." Roosuf said. "It is vital to all I have done and all I have." He stepped back, raising his arms in powerful sweeps to inscribe arcane patterns in the air while reciting chants in a language so old, and of such power, that the linguaring would not translate it; Wizard Tongue.

The air around the warrior and charger began to shimmer as if from waves of heat. "Do not fail, Gavilon," the wizard said. "The heir must be crushed if we are to flourish."

A final pass of his hands and the courtyard stood empty before him.

Roosuf nodded, then wheeled about and entered the sheltering darkness of the palace, leaving the daylight to creatures of suns and warmth.

Chapter Five

"Life is an illusion, but death is so damn real it can ruin your day."
T.K. Mitchell in the forward to his book, Pieces and Bits.

T.K. was trapped in the nightmare again. He knew it. He was very aware it was the nightmare, but with the inescapable fury of a monsoon he also knew he could not escape it and he was back in the jungle again.

The Jungle, green and red. Thunder of gunfire and yells of fear and pain. The smell of burning human flesh.

And the knife.

T.K. screamed in the nightmare and bolted awake.

He was covered in a cold sweat, the thermal undershirt he wore to sleep in sticking to him. He was lying on his right side, huddled in a fetal position and shivering.

Damn, he thought, *just once I'd like to make it through a whole night. I wonder if I have any Jack Daniels left.*

He rolled onto his back to sit up just as an axe thudded to the ground where his head had been.

Instinctively, T.K. doubled forward, throwing his body away from the axe man and kicked at the attacker with his right foot. The axe man screamed in pain and fell backwards clutching at his left shin.

T.K. rolled to his feet in a defensive crouch, still holding his walking stick. His tactical instincts took over, leaving him time for only one thought: *What the hell is going on?* Beyond the axe man, the earthman could see other shapes materializing out of the darkness. He stopped counting at nine.

"Damn," he mumbled.

He allowed his attention to wander toward Lord Shoutte's bedroll just long enough to see more dark forms surround it. "Shoutte!" T.K. yelled but it was too late. Half a dozen attackers descended in a blinding flurry of slashing blades and hacked the dark shape of the bedroll to pieces.

"Bastards!" T.K. cursed. Then he dismissed Shoutte and compartmentalized his grief in favor of survival.

"Alright, you sons-of-bitches," he whispered, "you're not gonna take me that easy."

The attackers began to circle T.K., drawn swords and axes reflecting the sudden cold moons' light. T.K. took a relaxed stance and slowly turned in place, careful not to focus on any one particular assailant. He kept his eyes focused inward and relied on peripheral vision to warn him of the first advance from the circle's perimeter.

In the meantime, he grasped his walking stick just off center with both hands and gave it a quick twist. The stick separated into two sections, becoming two arnis bastons—used in the Filipino stick fighting art—one thirty inches and the other twenty inches. Each had a metal cap at the end, the tip and cap of the cane. Holding each stick by the uncapped end, he kept them moving constantly in front of him in an upper eight pattern, ready for any move from the circle.

While most of the bandits watched the bastons with moth-to-flame fascination one of the attackers lunged at the earthman's exposed back. T.K. perceived the movement in time and shuffled to the left kicking twice with his right leg.

He broke the kneecap of the man while at the same time striking across the bridge of the man's nose with his right baston and shattering the bandit's left elbow with the left baston. Then T.K. turned to race for the gap in the circle.

Those around the fallen bandit closed in but T.K. was already out of the circle, maneuvering for better terrain. Using 'close ground' technique he parried a lance thrust from one bandit who tried to bar his way.

He blocked with both sticks then stepped in toward the startled bandit to strike at his hands and 'climb his body' with lightning-fast multiple strikes like a maddened drummer beating out a rhythm of death.

The metal tips of the bastions, moving in excess of eighty miles an hour, impacted on the bandit's hand, throat, collarbone, cheek, and finally his temple, killing him instantly.

The earthman found an area of open ground, piles of rubble and twisted brush created a maze of obstacles, which he used to narrow his opponents' lines of attack. T.K. avoided a saber cut at his head from a man charging in from behind him by dropping and pivoting on his left knee so the blade passed harmlessly over him.

His right baston came out of its chambered position like a rattlesnake's tongue and struck up to shatter the bones of the swordsman's hand. He second struck to shatter the elbow, X-blocked to re-break the wrist and then, as the man howled in pain, T.K. rose to strike him in the back of the skull with the butt end of one stick to render the man unconsciousness. T.K. grabbed the sagging body and sent the bandit into the oncoming path of two others as he jumped to his feet.

T.K. whirled in a quick circle ready for the next onslaught, but the bandits had backed off to reassess.

The night sounds seemed to have disappeared. The only noises that competed with T.K.'s pounding heart for his attention were the moans of the wounded men.

T.K. took his first good look at the band of men trying to kill him and gave a tight, grim smile. To a man, the dozen were tough, seasoned fighters who could never be fooled twice with the same trick.

These guys give ugly a whole new meaning, T.K. thought. The attackers all bore scars of past combats—an ear partially bitten off, an eye patch, a hook hand. *Man, they make the Hell's Angels look like Mouseketeers.* Most of the intruders wore leather tunics of one sort or another, scaled or with metal rings sewn onto them. Some wore pieces of metal armor; greaves, helmets, a chest plate, or chain mail. All were armed with deadly weapons they were comfortably familiar with.

T.K. revolved slowly, taking in every movement, no matter how small, of the men around him.

His bastons were held loosely in his hands and shivering in an X before his body, never still, as if hungry for more contact with his enemy's flesh. *One way or another this is all gonna be over real quick*, T.K. thought. *And no matter how many I clock the rest are gonna cut me to pieces.*

A bearded swordsman to his left drew back for a slash at T.K.'s legs but the earthman stepped back with his left leg, removing his body at a forty-five degree angle from the blade's path. He took out the sword hand with his right stick and then switched his feet to step to the bandit's right.

The left *baston* snapped to the temple, the right to the right eye; the left re-struck from under T.K.'s right armpit to smash into the man's throat in a"broken six" move. He finished the man with a thrust of his left *baston* to the man's sternum and then jumped across the fallen body to put it between him and the next nearest man.

The entire sequence had taken less than ten seconds.

T.K. shook his head to clear sweat from his eyes. His skin tingled with the heightened sensitivity of combat and he fought the natural human impulse to panic at the odds against him by forcing a relaxed breathing rhythm.

One scum at a time.

The attackers hesitated for a second time, stunned by the explosive efficiency of his combat technique, unsure of which one of them wanted to test him for the next trick.

He allowed himself a wry smile.

So much for dying in bed between Annette and Sandra Dee.

He readied himself for a final charge and picked what he decided were the two ugliest members of the band: the axe man who had first attacked him and a brute whose only garment was a kilt made from a single, strange animal skin.

You two are my final service to the world of women, he thought with a sneer. *Some ladies will never know how lucky they'll be not to meet you.*

Suddenly, from somewhere in the distance, an inhumanly high-pitched howl ripped through the night. It penetrated to the core of every man at the ruins and a shudder went through them. It sounded like a tormented soul crying for release.

The cry froze everyone in their tracks and was followed almost immediately by an equally distant very human scream of pain, which ceased abruptly.

In a moment the group shook off the effects of the cries and began to move in again.

Keep a lamp in the window, T.K. thought to the distant screamer, *I'll be along to join you in hell directly.*

+++

Olzen Mar-Kamot of Tolan was rapidly finding that the life of a country bandit was losing all its charm. The nights were cold, the days were hot and dusty, he was bored and the money of late had not been very good.

Olzen, a tall, thin, handwringing sort of man with sad brown eyes, had been assigned, with two of the others, to watch the bandit gang's mounts while the rest of them went to kill the outworlder and the priest.

It was a boring but safe job. Olzen liked safe.

It was the reason that he and his business associate, Jonzun Laquand Moot had fled Ell'ena and ended up in the wilderness. A transaction had gone sour and they decided the country air would be healthier.

The two had stolen two vorn and fled east to avoid a confrontation with dissatisfied customers, but their luck had gone from bad to worse. They were set upon by Axe's band of cutpurses and had to choose between death or joining the gang. Jonzun was becoming convinced they had made the wrong choice.

"I can't stand another of Skin's hideous meals, Jonzun," he complained. "We have got to do something about it. I'm not at all sure last night's dinner was completely dead."

Jonzun was a stout man, half a head shorter than Olzen, but twice his girth. He had a cherubic face and short, red curly hair, which was marred above the left ear by a burn-scarred bald spot—a souvenir of a bordello fire in Umbria.

"Oh, stop your prattling!" Olzen commanded, "At least they're still feeding us. We wouldn't be in this mess if you'd bothered to get your facts straight."

"It wasn't my fault," Jonzun said, "That merchant was supposed to be away two moons cycles."

"But he wasn't, was he? He came back, found out we had sold his whole warehouse of Thorangian rugs and set the city guard on us!" Olzen raised his voice and the mounts picketed in the stand of trees all whinnied in fright.

"Now see what you did with your bellowing!" he added, and went over to quiet them.

"Help me shut these stupid beasts up or they'll bring that whole tribe of those filthy Svora down on our heads."

The others of the brigand group had left the vorn in this stand of trees just over the rise from a band of nomadic Svora. They then walked the quarter mile to the warp orphan's camp, lest the skittish mounts give them away.

A bulky shape in leather scale armor lurched down the hill and startled the two reluctant bandits. Beljor had been left behind with Jonzun and Olzen because of an unhealed sword wound in his side... and to watchdog the two of them.

"Keep those mounts quiet, you idiots," Beljor ordered, "Those Svora seem to be staying close to their fires, but we don't need to invite them to visit us here!"

Jonzun and Olzen walked the line, soothing each beast with a few words and a pat on the muzzle.

"Stinking beast," Olzen whispered.

"Oh, they're not so bad," Jonzun said,

"Have you ever been near a wild vorn herd? They roll in the mud and that makes one foul smelling animal."

"No, you tvek-headed Belisian, I meant Beljor stinks."

"Oh, then I agree with you on that point, he is foul."

"If I thought we could get even a half a mile before he caught up with us..." Olzen mumbled. Jonzun nodded solemnly.

Suddenly there was an inhuman wailing and then a very human scream from up the hill.

"Beljor!"

The two bandits raced toward the sound, completely out of character and drew their swords.

"What are we doing?" Jonzun asked as he jiggled along.

"I want to know what is going on," Olzun said, puffing. "This could be some trick to test our loyalty."

It was not; several minutes later they found Beljor and by then it was too late to prove anything to him. The bandit was dead, his body a gory mess, ripped almost literally to pieces by some animal.

Jonzun and Olzen were both violently ill for some time.

Both recovered their wits and enough health to run for their mounts when the inhuman wailing was repeated from over the hill in the Svora camp.

"What do we do?" Jonzun asked as he gasped for breath at the bottom of the hill. He kept looking up at the top of the hill expecting a hell mouth to open any minute.

"Ride," Olzen answered, equally breathless. "And take the other mounts so Axe and the rest can't follow." He began to un-tether the nearest vorn.

"You are a wise man, my friend," Jonzun said. "And these vorn'll bring a fair price in Tolan," he added with a smile, "as fair compensation for our interrupted journey with these demons."

Olzen smiled as he mounted. "I knew there was a reason I partnered with you, Jonzun Laquand, a solid business head to go with my loose morals." The two men laughed as they rode off ignoring the screams from the Svora camp and the inhuman cries of triumph that followed.

+++

T.K. never made it to Axe or Skins to perform his last service for the ladies of the world of Altiva. As he took his first step forward there was a startled cry off to his left and two bandits dropped. Both men showed the dragon-carved handle of a throwing knife projecting from the base of their skulls.

The remaining bandits were thrown into confusion by this new development. T.K. used the opportunity of the diversion to whirl and head away from where the two bandits fell.

The nearest bandit took a machete swing at T.K. but the earthman struck the man's hand with one baston and shattered his jaw with the other. T.K. never broke stride, racing away from the circle of death.

He headed for the mounts, but two of the faster moving bandits were already moving to cut him off, so he changed course. He chose to put his back to a long low wall to make his second last stand.

The bandits were now closer together in a semi-circle facing him. "Aren't you guys getting tired of standing around me yet?" T.K. asked. "I really have nothing worth taking."

"You've got your head," one of the men said with a cruel laugh. "That's worth more than enough to Roosuf."

T.K. was startled by the familiar name but it was overshadowed by the shock the bandits exhibited when Lord Shoutte exploded out of the darkness behind them.

The priest held the great crystal sword Rhythemwand above his head, his elbows bent outward. He waited in silent challenge; three bandits turned to answer it.

Abruptly Shoutte advanced like a juggernaut, the sword describing a crimson arc down to the left through the closest bandit. The priest followed through on the stroke and then stepped back with his right foot, drawing with all his might on the sword to torque it in a sweeping horizontal slash.

Rhythemwand cleaved through the second attacker and his shield, neatly bisecting the man. The startled bandit watched his own legs continue the charge and screamed as his torso fell to the ground in a pool of feces and intestines.

The third attacker was already inside the radius of Shoutte's swing, driving hard with his shield to smash the priest off his feet. He held a hand axe drawn back ready for the killing blow.

Shoutte tried to spin out of the way but could not avoid all of the force of the shield's concussive blow. The air was knocked out of Shoutte but the bandit had outmaneuvered himself; his momentum carried him a step beyond the priest.

Shoutte reacted quickly, reversing his grip on the sword and spinning to the left. The slash all but severed the out flung axe arm and sliced along the lower back of the shield rusher.

A fourth attacker moved at Shoutte before the priest could recover his balance, but T.K. leapt in with a simultaneous baston hit and a kick, which disabled the bandit.

It was too much for the bandits. Axe yelled to his men to "make for the mounts" and, almost as suddenly as they had come, the bandits were gone, carrying their wounded with them.

The sudden stillness that came over the camp only heightened the pounding of blood in T.K.'s head. Adrenaline fatigue set in and he found himself sitting on a piece of rubble because his legs would no longer support him.

Fragments of the nightmare came unbidden: the dripping knife, the smile, and the scream. T.K. shivered.

"Tee-Kay," Lord Shoutte said in his hoarse whisper, "Are you alright?" The Kovar priest massaged his bruised left shoulder and flicked Rhythemwand once to clean the gore from it, then wiped it on the tunic of one of the dead bandits to clean off the last of the blood.

"Oh, yeah," T.K. said with sudden violence in his voice, "I love to spend my evenings with the boys." He pulled his eyes away from the crystal sword as Shoutte clicked it into its sheath.

"Just what the hell was that all about?" T.K. yelled as he struggled to his feet and limped over to the hacked-up bedroll.

"Brigands, it would seem." Lord Shoutte extracted his throwing knives from the two dead bandits and began a systematic search of all the rest, making sure each was dead before moving on to the next.

"No," T.K. said, "this." He kicked at the hacked-up bedroll and a hastily fashioned dummy of brush and harness was revealed.

"If you knew they were going to attack, why didn't you warn me?" He realized he was trembling with a mixture of rage, fatigue and delayed fear.

"I heard the cry of the ko-ta bird." Shoutte said. "They are not usually heard this far east. I became suspicious, so I put out the fire and slipped away in the darkness to investigate."

"Why the hell didn't you make a move sooner?" T.K. forced himself to sit down and took off his right sock, careful not to rip it on any exposed screws.

"There were two more brigands in the woods," Shoutte said, his attention drawn to T.K.'s foot. "I was—eh—delayed by them."

The brilliant moons-light gleamed off the duralumin and surgical steel creation that replaced T.K.'s right foot. There was a support brace on either side of the ankle that ran to a leather collar strapped around his lower calf.

"Damn tension on this thing," T.K. cursed, "always needs readjusting." He fussed with the brace and stamped the foot a few times until he was satisfied with it.

"You have learned to conceal it well," Lord Shoutte said. He picked up the two bastons T.K. had dropped and examined them.

"Oh, mostly I just ignore it. A souvenir of my time in 'Nam."

"That war field you spoke of to me as we rode today?"

T.K. nodded, working hard to hold back memories; it had been a while since he'd had the nightmare during his waking hours. He expected he'd have a whole new wave of them after the violence of that night. It always came in waves, especially when the alcohol ran out.

Shoutte sensed T.K.'s mood and quickly changed the subject. "You are full of surprises, Tee-Kay. Like these." He clicked the *bastons* together to form the walking stick. "And the way you fought. I have never seen the like and I have studied martial arts of many sorts all my life."

"It's called arnis or kali," T.K. replaced his sock and rose to take the walking stick from Lord Shoutte. "I'm not very pure with it anymore, but I studied with some very good teachers in Malibu and on my first tour, over in the Philippines." Then he added with a sad smile, "It gets the job done."

Shoutte went to the pile of gear that had been off loaded from the pack animals. He rummaged until he found a folding spade.

"I must see to these men," Shoutte said, "or we will be overrun with scavengers before the dawn."

"Hang on, Shoutte. I'll give you a hand." The priest produced a folding shovel for him. "Funny, I never thought of graves registry as a luxury before," T.K. mused. "But everything is relative, right?"

It took the two men just over an hour to bury the bandits. They found a shallow gully just outside the ruins and carried the bodies to it, then filled

"YOU HAVE LEARNED TO CONCEAL IT WELL,"

it in with rubble and earth.

Both kept a watchful eye on the trees and one hand on their weapons, but there was no sign of returning bandits. The hour was spent in silence, partially because of the need to be alert for an attack and partially because of the grimness of the work.

T.K. fought nausea at the smell and sight and the insistence of the nightmare the entire time. He kept seeing all the graves he'd seen when his father made the monuments and then all the body bags in the jungles filled with the pieces of his warrior brothers, sometimes not even enough to call it a full body. He shivered more than once while he dug, but not from any chill air.

Finally, the last stone was piled on the mass grave and Shoutte murmured a whispered prayer, a strange sound that was half rasped and half a song heard distantly. The words were indistinct but T.K. caught 'transition,' 'journey' and 'cycle before the priest concluded with "To the Rhythem."

Then the cleric made a marker out of a tree branch. On the marker he etched the same triple diamond symbol as was on his chest with a chalk-like rock. "We dare not risk a funeral pyre here," he said, remorsefully. "A remembrance stone will have to do."

"My old man spent his whole life cutting grave markers out of granite and marble," T.K. said. "Could have been a real sculptor, had the talent, but he said, 'Teel, there is a need to be filled. My art is you and your brother and my love for your mother.'" The earthman turned away from the grave with a deep sigh.

"He was a wise man," Lord Erique Shoutte said. "We must each fill a need in the rhythm of things. That is the Rhythem."

"I wonder about that. I've learned a lot about need since 'Nam. I kind of figure it's all a joke anyway, either you get the punch line or you are the punch line."

"The Rhythem is difficult to see sometimes but if one perseveres it can be found. Though sometimes the vision must be turned inward to see that way."

T.K. set his shovel down and rummaged in his pack for the Jack Daniels bottle. There was only a mouthful left and he swilled it with quiet joy, prolonging the taste as long as possible.

"The Sioux have a ceremony called the Vision Quest," he swallowed the last mouthful. "A young brave goes away from the tribe and fasts and prays in the mountains until a spirit guide comes to him in a vision and puts order to things for him. Sort of acts like a tour guide to his actions."

He dropped the empty bottle into the pack with a longing expression. "This is the only spirits I've ever run across, the only guide I've had in looking for a place to call home. And I ain't ever had that."

Lord Shoutte began removing the ceremonial robes that he had donned for the bandits Transition Ceremony at the grave. "It is never easy; no one gives us an answer, and even often when we find the answers we do not recognize them," he folded the robe and took a drink from a wineskin among the gear. "But perhaps your visit here will help you to find some answers."

"Ah, who the hell knows? I'm not even sure what questions to ask." He shrugged his shoulders and picked up his walking stick and cast a hooded look at the priest. "I'll take the first watch."

"You doubt my alertness?" Shoutte sounded genuinely hurt.

"Let's just say I'm worried about you taking a walk in the woods." T.K. grabbed a 'horse' blanket from the gear and threw it around his shoulders. Then he smiled with a sudden thought.

"You can use my sleeping bag, Erique," he said with a laugh, "since yours looks like Swiss cheese."

Shoutte was about to make a sharp reply when the inhuman wail that they had heard during the fight sounded again, more distant than before, but no less haunting.

T.K. shrugged again. "Another lost soul. At least we're not alone."

The earthman took up a position with his back to the junction of two low walls so he could keep watch on the animals and the sleeping form of the priest. He did is best not to let his mind wander, to think back to so many night watches in-country. He tried not to imagine 'Cong beyond the treeline.

Stay here, he admonished himself whenever his mind started to wander toward The Nightmare. *That jungle is in the past. Leave it there.*

He woke the priest after two hours and tried to sleep, being only halfway successful. There were no further incidents during the night and, despite the interrupted rest, both men were awake at dawn and anxious to be away.

T.K. observed that the Younger Brother, the smaller, bluish sun, rose and set an hour (by his internal clock's guess) sooner than its larger, pinker counterpart. It allowed two hours a day when the shadow agreed with T.K.'s earthborn sensibilities.

It helped him adjust.

The first hour in the saddle with Lord Shoutte as company was pleasant. Neither man pointedly made mention the violence of the night before.

They spoke little, allowing T.K. to drink in the lush scenery. He saw a number of squirrel-like creatures, ten different varieties of birds and numerous varieties of shrubs and trees with leaf colors that ranged from green/blue to indigo.

He saw one bush far rarer than the others colored a bright aquamarine tinged with crimson on the leaf tips. Lord Shoutte called it a thodist bush and said it was a powerful poison. They stopped at one of the thodist bushs whose leaves, unlike the other, were almost entirely red.

"It is a deadly poison at all times," the priest lectured, "but when it is seeding, as this one is, with the proper care it is an excellent pain reliever." The priest set about plucking the reddest leaves and then noticed T.K.'s odd expression.

"My training has been in all the Transition Arts," the priest explained, "from life to death." He touched the saber at his hip to make his point, "and ill to well."

"You're a doctor too, Erique?"

"A healer? Yes. As I said before, we all fill a need for someone else. I was trained as a Priestsinger, healer, and warrior at the Academy Kova many years ago and still return there to teach and to study, for there is always more to learn."

He touched the triple diamond brand on his chest and T.K. began to understand his companion was indeed more complex than he had first supposed.

They camped temporarily beside the red bush so that Shoutte could grind some of the leaves into paste form to store for later use as medicine. T.K. wandered away from the camp to the top of the next hill to look at the countryside ahead and made a horrifying discovery near a sight that had obviously been some sort of camp: the horribly mutilated corpse of a human body.

"This must be the poor devil we heard last night," T.K. said once Lord Shoutte had been summoned. "Your world seems awfully full of death."

Shoutte nodded.

"There is death in every world, Tee-Kay. Perhaps my world simply has fewer illusions about permanence; why the Kova is the guiding principle of my life; it teaches me to accept these chances of state." Shoutte moved to his pack vorn to begin re-donning his red and blue ceremonial robe.

"You can take care of this burial detail by yourself this time," T.K. said.

"I'm suddenly tired of digging graves." He turned away in disgust, wishing he had another Jack Daniels bottle on hand.

"Even I will admit," Lord Shoutte began to dig a hole beside where the body was found. "That of late the number of transitions has been a little too frequent for my liking." He looked over at the mutilated corpse and made the diamond shaped prayer symbol of his fath with his hands.

"By the Rhythem," the cleric said, "what manner of beast could maul a man so?"

"It was the Shadowbeast." A new voice came from behind the two men.

Shoutte spun holding the shovel like a sword and T.K. whirled, snapping his walking stick in two.

The strange voice was that of an old man in a long white robe who was walking down the hill towards them.

His robe was emblazoned with three interlocking squares, in red, blue, and yellow. It reminded T.K. of Lord Shoutte's chest symbol. On sighting each other's symbols, Shoutte and the stranger performed stylized bows.

"The Rhythem fulfilled …" Shoutte began.

"—is the Rhythem begun," the stranger concluded. Behind the new arrival several young men and women appeared, dressed like the old man in long white robes but with only one or two squares on their clothing.

T.K. thought immediately of hash marks.

"I am Lord Erique Shoutte, my companion is Tee-Kay Mitchell, a warp orphan."

The old man regarded T.K. with distant amusement. "Oh, I see," he said with a gentle smile.

"Hi." T.K. extended his hand, but the old man didn't quite know what to make of the gesture.

"I am Tohfa of the Svora," the old man said. "Come, sup with us. My acolytes will bear the body to a pyre and prepare for its Transition Ceremony." He motioned to two of the young men standing nearby who hastened to comply.

"Others will see to your mounts." Tohfa turned without waiting for a reply and started up the hill leaning heavily on a walking stick.

Lord Shoutte looked to T.K. and nodded that it would be all right to follow. The two started after the old man at a slow walk.

"He's a priest like you, right?" T.K. whispered. Shoutte gave him a long suffering "oh, you poor, dumb heathen" look, but answered in a patient *sotto voce* tone.

"In a way. The Svora are a nomadic tribe which converted to the study of the Kova some years ago but were unwilling to part with certain confining customs of their ancestors." He made a pitying face. "They splintered the tenets to form a similar, but vastly inferior religion."

"Sounds like an old tune played a lot on my world as well, schism this and schism that," T.K. commented. "What—uh—confining customs, might I ask?"

"Oh, marriage for life, hereditary lifetime leadership, celibacy for priests." Shoutte shuddered at the very thought of the later. "Barbaric."

"Could give a fella headaches," T.K. said sympathetically.

"But the Rhythem allows all variations, however ghastly in concept. The Kova recognizes all religions and we who believe in it know that ultimately change will be apparent to all." Shoutte did his best to put on a pleasant face, and T.K. was reminded of a missionary entering headhunter country. He did his best not to laugh.

From the top of the hill the entire Svora camp was visible. There were more than a hundred wickiup-type structures arranged in a circle around a central clearing. Most of the wickiups were down to bare wooden frames, and it was obvious that most of the camp's population had already left, and hurriedly from the state of the space. What activity was centered in the clearing. As they moved closer, T.K. could see half a dozen acolytes gathered around.

"Most of our people left as the Elder Brother rose this morning," Tohfa led them down a broad 'street' which led toward the clearing and a dozen still-occupied wickiups. "The herd had to be moved away as quickly as possible."

"On what urgency?" Shoutte asked with real concern.

The old man sighed and his calm manner was replaced by a deeply pained expression. "For a second night in a row the shadowbeast attacked. This time two children, a herder, and four of the herd died by its cursed hands. The herd was moved to that before the sunset it will be a safe distance from this place."

"But what about your guys left behind?"

Tohfa smiled beneficently and patted T.K. on the shoulder. "We Svora depend for our food, our medicine, and our future upon the herd. The tribe's survival is far more important than we few who have stayed behind to perform out religious duties."

His smile faded. "We shall be safe in any case, since we can move faster than the main body of the tribe. We may be with them by nightfall."

The three men came to one of the occupied wickiups. There was a bubbling stewpot and a fire in front.

"This creature you call a shadowbeast," Shoutte said, "I have never heard of it nor seen such violence as what it did to that man before. What manner of creature is it?"

Tohfa motioned the two visitors to sit near the fire. He squatted cross-legged and they followed suit.

"We will sit and eat. Such things should not be discussed on an empty stomach." Nearby a number of mounts were tethered and there was a teenaged girl lashing packs to a travois. At the sound of the old man's voice the girl moved to the fire where she took wooden bowls and ladled stew into them for each of the men.

T.K. smiled broadly at the delicate boned, dark-haired girl as she handed him his bowl then shyly moved on to Shoutte. She made a second round passing out a tortilla-like bread with which to eat the stew. This time she answered T.K.'s smile with a giggle and a blush. All this was not lost on Tohfa, who perked up.

"My late brother's daughter, Iffa," he said with a shrewd smile. "Her bride price is only five Svor; she has poor eyesight."

T.K. almost choked on his stew and dropped his bowl. "I ah… most politely must decline, Reverend," he managed, "as I've neither the—"

"Svor—" Shoutte whispered, fighting an unmanly urge to snicker.

"Svor," T.K. continued, "nor the time. I'm passing through looking for a warp wizard."

"Pity," Tohfa said with resignation, "pity. I have to keep discounting her. She's almost thirteen turns, you know—a spinster! Are you sure?" He asked with a flame of renewed hope, "perhaps four Svor and two Tveks? She has good legs."

T.K. watched the girl loading some pack animals and found himself feeling the old creep for agreeing with the old priest's assessment of the young girl's legs. He gave a deep sigh and tried to find another way to gently turn the offer of matrimony down. *He perked up like a D.A.R. lady hitting bingo. I almost hate to disappoint him.*

Lord Shoutte quickly saved him by interjecting, "The shadowbeast, my colleague, you promised to tell us of it. I have never heard of such a creature."

"It is a creature of recent appearance, a thing from legends," Tohfa intoned as if truly recalling a nightmare. "Two turns ago it first appeared as we moved through this area to summer grazing. It killed six people that turn before we passed beyond its hunting ground."

"That doesn't sound right, from what I know of earth animals," T.K. said, "Once they become man-eaters, they'll follow a food source and stop being territorial." Both Shoutte and Tohfa seemed pleasantly surprised by his grasp of the situation.

"But this demon does not feed on its victims." The old priest elaborated. "It kills horribly as you saw with that stranger, leaving the remains for the scavengers but not feeding on the flesh. It is as if it is the terror and pain of the victim that nourishes it," Tohfa made a hand gesture which created a square—T.K. had seen Shoutte form a diamond with a similar steepling of the hand—and spit in an obvious curse. "It is a wizard creature."

"Stranger?" Erique exchanged a puzzled look with T.K. "You mean the man we found over the hill was not of your tribe?"

"Pff!" Tohfa said with humor. "Fansavs be damned, no! I suspect he intended us some harm but chose the wrong moment to approach our camp for theft or deviltry. There were several strange mounts in our herd today as well so I suspect he was not alone."

Shoutte considered for a moment. "Yes, I would venture he was of the band that attacked us last night at those nearby ruins of the Ashun temple."

Tohfa signaled to Iffa and she brought three ceramic bottles, each filled with an ale-like brew. T.K. took a cautious sniff and found the aroma refreshing.

"To the Rhythem," Shoutte proclaimed and gulped his.

"To the Rhythem," Tohfa said and chug-a-lugged his.

"Here's mud in your eye!" T.K. drank, coughed and gulped the rest of the cup.

The other two men stood up.

"Come," Tohfa said. "It is time to witness the Transition ceremony." T.K. jumped up to follow and was joined, several seconds later, by his stomach.

"Whew," T.K. whispered, "that stuff's got a kick that sneaks up on you." He caught up to the other two doing his best not to wobble and made a note to get the name of the potent brew.

The pyres at the central clearing were already aflame when the three men arrived. Twenty or so acolytes stood in a square around the pyres and watched the thick column of smoke snake skyward.

Tohfa smiled at the two travelers in invitation and then stepped into place in the square. He began a solemn yet joyous chant that was then picked up by the others.

"Somewhat like the plains tribes of my own world," T.K. whispered to Shoutte. "The smoke carries the spirit to the sky world paradise." The priest nodded and stepped forward. T.K. caught his arm. "Is attendance mandatory—will I offend them if I opt out?"

Shoutte shook his head, smiled, and stepped into the square. The beauty of the ceremony offset the horrors that the burning bodies conjured, but the odor was another matter. The smell of the burning flesh brought up the all too familiar miasma and threatened to trigger The Nightmare again for TK.

The young girl from Tohfa's wickiup appeared around the corner of another dwelling some distance ahead. She recognized T.K. and waved him to her. He reluctantly obeyed her summons, in part to get further away from the pyre smoke. He was within three meters of her when a thick column of smoke blew between them. He lost sight of her for a moment in the acrid cloud.

Wind must have changed, T.K. thought. I wonder what she wants. The smoke blew past and Iffa was no longer there. In her place was the old woman from the train and his vision: Meegana.

"You again!" he exploded with disgust.

"I will not be able to join you for some time," she said in a voice that seemed to come from all around him. "Be warned, Roosuf knows you are here. I sense his weather warpcraft beginning. He is calling a shadowstorm, against you."

T.K. stood aghast and just shook his head. "Lady, listen, I don't want to be on your world."

"Your world too, Teel, a world beset by great evil."

"Your problem lady," T.K. interrupted. "I don't want the job. Understand me? Good old earth has sex'n'drugs'n' rock 'n roll is all I want and can handle. That's evil I can relate to, not shadow beasts and mad wizards and all this magic show stuff."

"Be warned," she continued as if he had not spoken. "This, my warpcraft image cannot be maintained for long or Roosuf will be able to detect my energy and know where you are. He has agents everywhere." Her voice began to fade as if someone were turning down the sound on a T.V. "Beware shadows, Teel Kantos. They hide death and mark the sky wi—". Another cloud of smoke obscured the woman wizard for a moment and when it cleared the young girl was standing there again!

"Hey, wait." T.K. stepped closer to the girl and looked around frantically for the vanished wizard. "I don't want the job!"

"Oh, but sire," the young girl said, "Do not judge me on the surface alone. I am not so shapely but I am an excellent cook and have much pillow skill… in theory, anyway." She looked thoughtful, as if trying to remember a speech. "They say I will bear fine children for my line is very fecund."

T.K. had a hard time ridding himself of the image of the old woman and stared at the girl with a confused expression.

"I can sing too," Iffa insisted, "and I am training to be a healer like my brother is."

"That's nice, honey," T.K. said distractedly. "Why don't you just get along with puberty. Trust me—it ain't you, it's me. I gotta go get crocked." He turned and walked toward the pyres, leaving a very puzzled girl.

The former marine stayed at the outside of the smoke radius, walking around the village for some time, trying to interpret what the old woman— or the vision of the old woman—had said to him.

Her words unnerved him and he decided not to tell the priest about his encounter, since he was not even sure it had really happened or all of it was some shard of The Nightmare and his dislocation to the new strange world.

T.K. and Lord Shoutte stayed for the finish of the Transition Ceremony and the Svora's last meal at the campsite afterward. Then the two groups mounted up and rode out in separate directions.

"Where to now?" T.K. asked as they watched the travois of the Svor move to the south.

"I spoke with Tohfa of your situation," Shoutte replied, "and he agrees that the most likely place to find a warp wizard is in the city of Tolan, capital of this country, Cozen. It is not a seaport town, but the river allows for much travel and there are wizards in residence there. The town is outside of my parish, but not by far and is where the Academy Kovar is located. It is about time I stopped back for a refresher course, in any case, so I will ride with you as far as Tolan."

"Ah," T.K. smirked, "So you do observe some priestly customs like parishes?" Shoutte looked at him crossly.

"I observe all of them." He kicked his mount forward and T.K. followed yelling.

"Okay, okay, no offense!"

✦✦✦

It wasn't until about an hour later that the survivors of Axe's band found the tracks of the two men they were looking for.

"We'll never catch up to them," said a slender, fine boned man, whose weapon was an ancient broadsword he seemed too thin to lift. "They're riding, you know. And we are on foot, or have you not noticed?"

"We'll catch up to them alright," Axe said. "After what they did last night, I'll chase those two to the seventh hell if I have to do it walking over razors."

"But Roosuf wanted us to—"

"Damn him and all warp wizards," Axe cursed. "This is personal now." He raised his axe menacingly and pointed eastward. "Those two die. Now move."

"This way. I can follow the pair of tracks." Skins led the way and then Axe, limping slightly, followed. The five other survivors followed at an easy trot, with a reluctant Sword bringing up the rear.

Chapter Six

"It's not whether you win or lose that counts, it's whether you get caught cheating."
Timothy Quentin Locke (escape artist)

"You know, Erique," T.K. said, "a couple more mornings like this one and I might just get to like your Altiva. I'm still stuffed."

The two men had spent the morning fishing for large red catfish-like pond creatures called bot-bots. It had been a welcome break after the monotony of the previous day's ride. The two men had not mentioned the bandits nor the Svora encampment all the last day and the previous night's camp had been without incident.

It all seemed a distant memory in the warm double suns-shine as the two men lazed on a streams bank in the afternoon's warmth.

"There are even bigger bot-bots in the rivers around Tolan," Shoutte said. Both men had eaten their fill of the catch and Shoutte had added a powder to the leftovers that he said would preserve the fish for several days. Altivans apparently used the powder in preference to salt.

"How many days ride is this city, you figure?" T.K. was laying back and picking his teeth with a stiff blade of grass.

"If we don't stop to fish again we will be in Tolan in eight days."

Eight days exposed to Roosuf's men, T.K. thought, looking around at the broken terrain in the double suns-light. They have the home court advantage but I don't know if I should tell Erique. I'm not sure where his political position on this Emperor guy will be.

"You look concerned, Tee-Kay," Shoutte noticed the warp orphan's far away look. "Have you some appointment you've not told me about?"

"No, noplace special, no particular time," T.K. said. "No one to see, which is to say, my normal condition in life. I am becoming more accustomed to the double shadows but I'm still having trouble judging distances."

"Yes, I have heard some warp orphans have that difficulty," the priest smiled. "But I cannot imagine any other way to see the world."

T.K. tried to concentrate on the scenery but the encounter with the bandits kept replaying in his mind and he toyed with the idea of telling Shoutte about Meegana and the threat Roosuf's men posed but wasn't sure if the priest would believe him. *Hell, I don't even really believe it.*

"You ever hear of a guy named Roosuf?" T.K. finally asked in as nonchalant a voice as he could fake.

"The Mephistalian?" Shoutte made the Kova symbol then spit like Tohfa had when he mentioned the shadowbeast. "Why speak of such unpleasantness?"

"I heard the name back at the Svora camp."

"Mephan is an island to the west of the twin continents," Shoutte said reluctantly, "and it is a hungry, conquering empire, or it was in ages past. They sent armies to invade even my own home of Umbria—though there they were repulsed. Other countries were not so fortunate, even Cozen felt the crushing heel of the Mephan boot." He gave a slight smile, "But in the fullness of time, as is the Rythem, they over-extended themselves, many allied against them and the Empire was forced to draw back upon itself. For a time there was peace with them and their emperiors became... reasonable. It still exerts much economic power over much of the world. Its current Emperor is a wizard as well and has persecuted my people and used the economic might of his empire to oppress those he does not actually war upon. You will not find much love for Mephans in this country."

It was clear the priest found the subject distasteful. T.K. found himself working frantically to find a way out of the conversation when a commotion from a head of them saved him the trouble.

There were high-pitched shrieks coming from several very upset animals over the next hill. Shoutte identified that the sounds were coming from vorns like the antlered creatures they were riding.

The two men eased their own mounts to the crest of the road with caution to see what the commotion was from.

The shrieking vorns were hitched to a wagon that looked like to T.K. like a Gypsy Varna back on earth. The four-wheeled conveyance had strayed off the road and become trapped in mud. The mire, however, was not the cause of the animal's consternation.

Two mounted men were harassing the driver of the wagon. That driver was a heavyset middle-aged woman who was holding the two riders at bay with a string of invectives and a short whip.

T.K. and Shoutte watched for a moment with mild amusement, but when the tall, thin rider drew his sword to menace the woman on the wagon, T.K. said, "That's it!" and nodded to Shoutte. He then kicked his mount forward. He let loose with a blood-curdling shriek, which was somewhere between a Sioux war cry and Johnny Weissmuller on a bad day.

It worked.

The two attackers turned, saw T.K.'s charge and kicked their vorns to leave. The two would-be bandits stopped only to untie half a dozen vorns they had tethered nearby. Within moments only a descending cloud of dust remained to mark the two attackers' visit.

T.K. waited for Lord Shoutte before approaching the driver. The upset woman kept up the string of invectives but substituted the vorn team as targets. The beasts continued squealing until Shoutte rode by and soothed each one.

"Stay back, you brigands!" the woman yelled, brandishing her whip. "Be gone with you!"

"Thanks to you too, lady," T.K. greeted with his best nonthreatening smile.

The woman reconsidered for a moment. "If you're not a brigand, you're thanked. Now get about your business." She waved the whip menacingly and Lord Shoutte quickly snatched it from her grasp.

"You've no need of this with friends," he said in a bright whisper.

"Friends?"

"We're going to help you out of the mire," the Kovar Priest said.

"I hope that was a royal we," T.K. whispered.

"A priest's duty is to help the distressed," Shoutte explained, "to restore the Rhythem."

"Fine," T.K. said, "but I took a vow of apathy."

"I did not ask for your help," the wagon driver declared.

"Your situation speaks for you," Shoutte said.

She cast a venomous look at the pair as the cleric dismounted and moved to the front wheels. "Now be prepared to urge the team." He looked up and saw that the earthman was still mounted. "Tee-Kay?"

"And I swore I'd never volunteer again." T.K. dismounted, tied his mount off to the same bush Lord Shoutte had secured the pack animals on and took up a position on the opposite front wheel.

All the while the driver continued her mildly abated harangue. "You have no right to bother me; I don't care if you are a Kovar Priest. I don't want help. I'll get the wagon out myself. Shoo! Go away..."

Both men heaved against the wheels while the vorn strained, but to no avail. Next the duo forced loose wood around the wheel for traction but again had no result.

"Perhaps if we lighten the load?" Shoutte suggested.

"Sounds good to me," T.K. turned to address the driver, "Okay, sweetcakes, off you go." He helped down the now resigned woman, and together the three of them heaved against the wagon several times. It still would not budge.

"It's still too heavy, and there's nothing around here to use for a lever," said T.K.

"Perhaps if we lighten it some more?" Shoutte suggested. T.K. agreed and the two men moved toward the door at the back of the wagon.

"No!" the woman yelled. "Get away from there!"

"Keep your shirt on lady," T.K. began, "we'll just offload the wagon a bit then—"

The door to the wagon burst open and both men froze, unable to believe what they saw. "Holy Mother of Pearl," T.K. blurted. "This sure as hell isn't Kansas."

+++

The Tarnished Vorn was an inn in the waterfront section of Mephan City, the capital of the Mephistal Empire. It is only steps away from the broad river, the Mouth-of-Vendor, which gave the inland city access to the sea, two miles distant.

It was not the safest neighborhood for aristocrats to travel in as it had a reputation as a rough and ready area frequented by footpads. Thus, it was unusual to see anyone with wealth enough to risk losing it to the denizens of the night.

Yet within the quarter hour, half a dozen individuals whose cloaks, if examined closely, were too perfectly shabby and whose sandals were of too fine a workmanship to be common folk, passed through the ovar wood doorway of the inn. All had gone straight to an upstairs back room to be admitted by a whispered password.

The last figure admitted, a heavyset Ker Nok merchant with skin so dark it was near indigo, who was bald save for a braided wealth-lock, named N'ku, said, "We are all here, but Havros. He is late. Let us begin."

"We will wait 'til everyone is here, my good merchant," Meegana Rakkdon said with a stern voice. "What we decide will affect us all, so it is best that no one should be excluded."

At that moment, a soft knock on the door caused the five men and women in the room to fall silent. More than one had delved beneath a robe to caress a jeweled dagger.

"Liberty," a whispered voice said from the other side of the door and the bolt was slipped back to admit the last member of the conclave, Duke Arkano Havros.

"My apologies for my lateness," the thin aristocrat said, "but it is a longer walk from the warp crossing than I had estimated; I do not know this part of the old city well."

The Duke was silver-haired and middle-aged, a veteran of countless court intrigues who maintained a cheerful business-as-usual attitude regardless of chaos around him. He calmly doffed his dark blue cloak and greeted each member of the conspiracy as if they were long lost friends.

"You took the warp crossing?" Madame Yeshar asked with a shocked tone. She was a woman whose rawboned, rugged beauty seemed at odds with the delicacy of her gestures, until one discovered she was a Kovar-trained healer. "Why not announce to Roosuf that we are meeting here, or better still, invite him along for a drink downstairs in the tap room?"

"Dear lady," the duke smiled with no rancor, "if I had taken either ferry and been recognized that would have been the sure result. I often warp across to this side of the city on family business—we own several nekot mills and a shipping firm. Less suspicion will fall on my idiosyncratic walk to a quaint tavern than one would think."

"Then let us get on with this dark business of revolt." Ortan, master jeweler and head of the Crafts Fellowship, said. He was a pudgy man whose hands seemed too thick-fingered to craft anything but the crudest ornaments, yet almost all in the room wore examples of his exquisite skill with metal-working.

"Keep your voice down, jeweler," Madame Yeshar hissed. "Know you not that wizards have a thousand ears?" She looked around nervously.

"And a thousand fingers to plug those ears," Meegana said. "I placed this room in a local warp which Roosuf cannot detect the moment we all arrived here and opened it only for Duke Havros to enter. I cannot maintain it for long, but we will remain undisturbed a short while."

"What of Thorvanus and his guardsmen who defended our retreat at the last meeting?" N'ku asked.

"Dead," Havros said in a solemn voice. "Horribly dead."

"Did any of them talk?" the healer queried with a quiver in his voice.

"Thorvanus would not betray us," N'Ku said, "and his men never actually saw any of us."

"Then the heir is safe," Ortan stated, "and we are free to continue with our plans."

"The heir may not be safe," the duke said. "The Lord Gavilon has not been seen around the palace or city for three days. Rumor has it that the executioner warped for the north continent."

"We cannot make a move without the heir," Ortan said. "He is the only figurehead all factions will support in a coup against the wizard-emperor; we need that shadow of legitimacy. We need all the factions or we will not be strong enough to oppose the army."

"All is not lost," Meegana spoke and the conspirators focused their hopes on her. "I have been in contact with the heir. Fear not, he is currently safe. The reason I sent him where I did was that Roosuf could not reach him quickly. Travel to the north continent is difficult this time of year—only limited warp portals can be used and so he is beyond the immediate grasp of Rossuf, especially if that beast does not know the exact place I have sent him."

"Can he be brought back here quickly?" the duke asked.

"Quickly would do us no good." the female wizard said. "We are not ready yet to rise yet, you've said so yourselves. I see I must go to him and prepare him for what is to come so he can be aligned with our purpose."

"She is right," Ortan added. "The arms we have purchased cannot be here for two moon cycles and some bribes must still be paid out."

"The longer we delay the more strength Roosuf gains," Madame Yeshar said.

"Not so," Ortan said. "The unrest among the masses is growing. Roosuf's religious sanctions and the taxes against warp transactions bring new converts to our cause daily. His boot on the throat of the people is not gentle and their pleasures are not so plentiful that they can feel comfort with any new burdens."

"DID ANY OF THEM TALK?"

Duke Havros slapped the table softly and all eyes shifted to him. "My friends, all that we can do is being done. We must await the arrival of the heir. When that day comes, we must be ready—the populace's hate for the emperor must be encouraged—subtly—to be in a fever pitch."

"Then we are done for today," the old wizard said. "Let us leave as quietly as we came and I will contact you all in a ten-day."

The conspirators left the inn one by one, going separate ways to the ferries until only Duke Havros and Meegana remained.

"What are the real chances of keeping the heir alive until we are ready?" the nobleman asked.

"There are many hallways in the house of chance," the wizard said. "Sadly, the lad does not seem too bright. If I reach him before Roosuf's agents and we can school him in what is to be done, we may yet return sanity to the throne. If not..." she let the future speak for itself.

"Very well," the Duke said, "walk in the suns-light, good wizard and mind the shadows." Then he whirled his cloak over his shoulder and left the inn with the carefree stride of an innocent man.

"Sometimes the twins make mistakes in birthings," Meegana whispered as she watched Havros leave. "There goes he who should be emperor."

+++

T.K. worked real hard to keep his jaw from bruising a toe when it dropped at his discovery in the caravan wagon, for vying for space in the doorway of the wagon were four of the most exotic and exquisitely attractive women he had ever seen or dreamt of.

The winner of the doorway contest was by far the most exotic. She was tall, shapely, wide shouldered, well-muscled and covered with fur. Not wearing fur, rather, truly covered in powder blue fur the texture of peach fuzz.

As nearly as T.K. could see by her clothing—which was not a lot—she was covered from head to foot with the close blue fur. She had waist-long hair a shade lighter than her fur, growing from where hair usually grows on earth women.

As for her facial features, they were beautiful with high cheekbones, full lips and piercing, intelligent green-in-amber colored eyes. The only word that came to T.K.'s mind, when he could form a word, was stunning.

"Stunning" smiled seductively and said in a kittenish hiss. "Well, is one of you going to help me down?" The two men all but jumped the wagon steps with T.K. a fraction of a second faster.

Her hand was warm, her grip firm, and it was obvious she needed absolutely no help stepping down. She stood almost seven feet tall, but almost succeeded in projecting demure. Almost.

The next woman out of the wagon was a lean black woman, whose features were a deep bronze-cocoa color. Lord Shoutte assisted her to the ground. "Thank you," she said, "my name is Adriana."

"I am Ku'zn," T.K.'s blue furred Amazon said.

The two men stood entranced while the other two women stepped down unassisted. One was a full figured, pale skinned red head whose left eye socket was tattooed in pale blue, like an inverted raindrop, that was birthed in an asterisk on her left cheek. The other woman was small, and frail looking. She had almond shaped eyes, yellow bronze skin and was long-haired.

"My name's Lunit," the redhead said. "This little flower is—"

"Yomichico Tosofuntonat," the little one said in a low musical tone, "but you may call me Yomi."

All the women wore variants of the sarong, but the variety of ways with which they had used them to almost cover their bodies was an obvious delight to the two men. The women also wore identical crystal bracelets on their right wrists that looked as if they were too tight to be removed by slipping them off. T.K. could see no lock or hinges on them. In addition, Ku'zn wore a necklace of cut crystal and Lunit wore a brimmed hat that looked like an odd leftover prop from Breakfast at Tiffany's.

"Afternoon, fair damsels. I'm T.K." He did an elaborate bow then nudged Lord Shoutte who smiled and bowed formally.

"Reverend Lord Erique Shoutte of Shoutte, your humble servant, ladies."

"A Priest of the Kova?" Yomi asked.

Shoutte nodded with a proud smile.

"I once worked in a Kovar contract house—" Yomi said.

"These are not ladies," the irate driver of the wagon burst into the conversation, "these are my girls." T.K. and Shoutte looked at each other, looked at the women, looked at the driver, and looked back at each other again.

"A traveling—" Shoutte began.

"Whorehouse," T.K. finished. "Sort of an adult motel on wheels."

"Don't you get any ideas," the driver declared, picking up a substantial-looking stick. "We'll fight."

The blue furred Ku'zn laughed. "But not too hard, Orancha." The other women joined in the laughter.

"We... uh... shall now attend to your pleasantly lightened wagon," Shoutte said. He turned to head for the front of the wagon and noticed T.K. had locked eyes with Ku'zn.

"Come, orphan, we had better work up a sweat."

"I'm doin' just fine workin' up a sweat right here," T.K. said, "Just fine." This time everyone laughed, including the madame.

Madame Orancha's traveling contract house (as Shoutte called it) was bound for a mining town southward, along the same road that the two travelers were heading, so it was decided (by all but Orancha) that the two groups would travel together.

Once the wagon was extricated from the mire they set off again at a leisurely pace. T.K. and Lord Shoutte took turns riding point to scout for trouble. Actually, they took turns riding behind the wagon and chatting with the four women.

T.K. learned that, among other things, on Altiva the oldest profession was as an honorable one, as well as a lucrative one. It was the refuge of the unskilled, the poor, and the drought-stricken farmer.

"Why would anyone be ashamed of sex?" Lord Shoutte said to T.K. "It is natural and necessary. And when done correctly, quite pleasant."

"Got me on all of that, brother," T.K. said. "I don't know where my mind was."

In grammar school, actually, he thought. *Thank goodness that is past.*

All the women in Orancha's establishment had been contracted to her service, an indenture of varying duration, because of some family—or, in Lunit's case—personal debt. None of the women thought of themselves as in any way shamed because of their status, though this was as much due to their character as the rigid rules which governed contract interactions.

When the twilight, created by the setting of the blue Younger Brother, came upon the group, they selected a hilltop close to a small stream and the pond it emptied into to camp.

Lunit and Adriana began setting up the kitchen while T.K. and Yomi gathered wood. Orancha kept them in sight at all times. Shoutte and Ku'zn tended to the mounts, picketing them between the trees.

The wagon was placed at the apex of a triangle with the picket line forming the base. The fire was set dead center of the space and brush and rocks and dirt were thrown up in a makeshift earthwork.

It was a good defensible position if things required it.

Custom demanded that the contractors and the two men eat from separate pots, but they used the same fire and shared ingredients. T.K. called the resulting meal was a Bot-Bot Mulligan stew.

Lord Shoutte passed his wineskin around, contributing to the festive atmosphere.

"I feel like I'm at a beach movie," T.K. said, to everyone's complete lack of understanding.

"You are a strange one, Tee-Kay," Ku'zn said, "but an interesting one, I think."

"I don't want to be nosy, Peachfuzz," T.K. said as he pulled out a notebook to sketch the post-dinner group, "but I'm the new Dorothy on the block. Are there many more like you at home?"

Yomi laughed. "Oh, there are no more like our Ku'zn."

"But my people, the Z'n are all furred like I am… if that is your question."

"Are your people the only fuzzy folk here on Altiva?"

"That I know of."

T.K. smiled when the others around the fire agreed with the Z'n. "I think you're kinda unique anyway, Peachfuzz." He accepted the wineskin from Lord Shoutte and sipped some of the Altivan wine. It was deep blue in color and tasted like cognac.

I like it.

"You should meet my brother, Ka'wn," Ku'zn said. "You would like him. You and he have much the same manner of humor."

"Ah," T.K. said, "crazed." He handed her the skin. "You wouldn't like my brother; V.J. is the original bad seed, a scum bum from the word go. I'm the one who told him to get lost eight years ago, now look at me—as lost as a little lamb could be."

The group sat and talked late into the night. By then the slightly tipsy Orancha decided it was time for her girls to get some beauty rest and she hustled them into the wagon, locking the door behind them.

"You know," T.K. set out his bedroll, "I could get to like this place. The booze is good, the ladies fair and I'm really no poorer than I was on earth."

"I have found it a world with as much to commend as to condemn in the Rhythem's ever changing flow," Shoutte said, "but then I have no other world to compare it to."

"Oh, there are places on earth as pretty, even in some cases as strange— but barring a complication I'd rather not get into—this place has promise." T.K. smiled oddly. "I could dig a place without cars and jets and factories. Just as long as I can get blitzed on wine like that and look at ladies like those, I'm happy."

"Is that all that matters to you?"

"What else is there?" T.K. asked in a quiet voice. "Oh, I used to think that maybe once there was. I tried marriage once after I came back from 'Nam, but she didn't deserve me. She was too nice a kid." He took off his boots and slid off the buckskin pants he had been wearing.

"Everything sort of sours for me after a while, you know?" He continued, "I get bored real easy with life and I don't seem to fit in anywhere. Not that I ever did, really. I thought I was fighting for something when I went into the corps, but when I got home I got spit on. Spit on. And with things that—that come back to me from the jungle I just could never fit back in. I guess 'Nam just made me more 'me' ya know? Made my skin a little thinner with all I… uh… saw there."

"I have seen violence too," Lord Shoutte said with a dark whisper of understanding. "My contract mate died at the hands of the men who did this." He ran his fingers along the prominent scar on his throat. "They made their transition months later at my hand, each and every one of them." He spoke without sadness at the memory but a certain quiet nostalgia showed through. "The only constant, my friend, in this life, is change. The principle my life is dedicated to. The Rhythem, the natural ebb and flow of life must be accepted."

When the earthman merely mumbled, "Sure," the priest gave an indulgent grin.

"Tomorrow, you will meet a family," Shoutte said. "Their oldest daughter died from the century plague three turns ago and it was not an easy passing. They loved her, but they accepted Janries' loss with grace which did her honor. The Kova must be accepted—in truth we have no choice."

There was silence. The two men wrestled for a moment with their memories.

"You know, Erique," T.K. finally said. "You really are a preacher after all. Wake me in three or four hours for my watch."

He rolled over, pulled up the covers and was snoring in seconds.

+++

The morning was glorious; the suns were hot, but a salty breeze from just over the eastern range of hills made it perfect weather for a dip in the pond. Orancha sat on the shore with her whip in her lap and a scowl on her face while the others splashed in the water, giggling. The six swimmers frolicked like children, tossing double entendres, but mostly with innocent frivolity.

Afterward the group took to the road.

It was a leisurely ride spent in idle discussion, jest, and song. T.K. produced a harmonica, Lord Shoutte a small device not unlike a juice harp, and Ku'zn blew forth on what for all intents and appearances was a bagpipe.

Lunit proved to have a beautiful singing voice and, both with accompaniment and a cappella, sang dozens of songs, a good portion of them bawdy.

T.K. had the strange feeling of familiarity with the whole circumstance, as if he was returning to a place he had known in a dream. It was a strange feeling, considering two suns, sword-toting villains, blue furred women and all, but nevertheless there was a familiarity and comfortableness about his time on Altiva. It was like he had stepped into a dream he did not remember he'd had, or maybe a memory of a place he'd been on a bender and forgotten.

This wouldn't be so bad a place, if I didn't have this empire thing hanging over me, he thought. If I sign papers of abdication maybe Roosuf will call off the dogs.

T.K. adjusted Whitefawn's gift vest and shifted on his mount. He wore his buckskin pants again, having made the decision to save his blue jeans for his return to earth. He could make new buckskin pants again if his stay on Altiva were a long one; his blue jeans would have to be his formal wear.

T.K. laughed out loud at the memory of a trip to Russia he had taken with his high school class. He'd been offered five hundred dollars for his jeans by a "citizen" who was probably a KGB operative trying to trap him.

Maybe I'll start Altiva's designer jean craze, he mused, *"Put a bum on your butt" will be the motto!* He laughed again at his own joke and completely put the violence of his time on Altiva out of his mind.

"What is so funny?" Orancha said from her perch on the wagon. "It will be dark soon. Just how far is this farmhouse, priest?"

"Just over the next rise," Lord Shoutte said. "A good Kovar couple that settled down to Storm Coast farming. They have two lovely young ones," he said, smiling. "Maybe three by now. Beokta, the wife, weaves like an Orandian elf. She made my blue dress mantle—the warmest cloak I ever—" Shoutte went rigid with horror.

The Kovar priest had fallen back so that he was riding beside the wagon team. T.K. was just behind him, so when the ridge was topped all three came in sight of the farm at the same time.

The farmhouse was a hollowed-out hill with a rounded doorway which stood open, with a still form sprawled face down lying half outside.

"Stay here 'til I signal," Shoutte commanded in his rasping whisper. He spurred his mount forward and drew Rhythemwand.

"What is it?" Ku'zn asked, poking her head out a small window on the side of the wagon. "Why are we stopping?"

"Trouble." T.K. said, "More damned trouble." He slipped his walking stick out of a carry strap on the back of the saddle and laid it across his lap with a horrible foreboding. His eyes stayed glued on the priest who had dismounted some yards from the farmhouse and was approaching in a cautious crouch.

The four women started to exit the wagon but Orancha shooed them back inside. "I most certainly do not like the look of this," the madam said.

T.K. held his breath for a long moment when Erique entered the hill house; he knew there was no way he could help the priest in a timely way should there be trouble waiting inside the building.

You should have backup, Erique, T.K. thought. *No solo recon patrols. There are no old bold heroes.*

The Kovar Priest emerged an eternity later clutching dizzily at the doorframe. He motioned the group forward with a weak gesture.

"One way or the other," T.K. said between clenched teeth, "we'll find out what's up now." He kicked his mount ahead and had dismounted before it came to a full stop by the house. Close up Lord Shoutte looked deathly white and shaken. "Erique, are you alright?"

"The shadowbeast," Shoutte whispered softly. His face was pale and bloodless.

T.K. knelt beside the body in the doorway to examine it with a premonition of horror.

The corpse had been a middle-aged man, now slashed almost literally to ribbons, his chest cavity gaped open, disemboweled. His face was a gentle, kind man's, who had spent his life close to the earth, exposed to the elements, and was virtually untouched by violence—except that his features were frozen in an expression of unbelieving shock and horror. He had died before he had a chance to feel pain.

The smell of the eviscerated corpse was overpowering even in the open air.

T.K. looked at Shoutte with a questioning expression.

"Even the children," the priest added with a weak whisper. The earthman looked into the dark interior of the house and could just barely make out the gory remains of three more bodies spread around the large main room.

A wave of nausea overwhelmed T.K. and he forced himself to turn away from the sight. He squeezed his eyes closed and fought for control. It was as if he had fallen into a deep pit; the sounds of the mounts, of the women exiting the wagon, and of Lord Erique Shoutte being sick beside him were distant and muffled. A great blackness engulfed him and he was on the verge of passing out. It was like The Nightmare was crawling into his skin and mind again.

Then the gunfire from The Nightmare started. *Once again his Armalite kicked in, then Duk's captured AK 47 began to spit fire at him.*

T.K. snapped his eyes open and saw Rhythemwand gleaming in Lord Shoutte's hand a few feet away. The earthman shot to his feet.

"Put that butcher's tool away," he yelled, then lurched off, unable to fight the nausea any longer.

The women from the wagon approached the farmhouse, but Shoutte motioned them back. "This is for me to deal with," he saw the concern in Ku'zn's eyes as she looked after T.K. "Go to him." She nodded and followed the earthman around the farmhouse.

"Shall we begin a pyre, priest of the Kova?" Yomi asked in a reverent voice.

"No," Lord Shoutte answered with a pained tone. "Their home will be their pyre."

T.K. found a quiet spot to be sick among some stunted trees behind the farmhouse. For several minutes his body and his mind were engulfed in the red-tinged nightmare. After he lost all his breakfast, all that were left were dry heaves and sobs.

That was how Ku'zn found him, huddled in the shadow of an angular rock. He was crying. She knelt and held him tight to her bosom until he had no more tears left.

"You'll get in trouble with your den mother," T.K. managed when the sobs had passed. His eyes were red-rimmed and his color was sickly white.

She still held him against her, the warmth of her fur and the gentle rhythm of her breathing were both soothing and arousing. "I don't want to get you birched for collaboration with the enemy."

"Orancha makes much noise," Ku'zn ran her fingers through his shaggy grey tinged hair. "But I've not violated any contract with her. You and I haven't gotten that far—" yet." She smiled with mischief. "Yet." T.K. laughed in spite of himself.

"You're something else, lady," he said. "The best mix of Ann Margaret and a teddy bear I can imagine." She regarded him with a puzzled expression.

"You are a strange one, Grizzlebeard."

"Yeah, Peachfuzz, that's my fame." He felt no compulsion to leave her comforting embrace. The cold splinters of The Nightmare had melted with her touch, but he knew it would be there waiting at the shadow edge of his next sleep. Or the next encounter with death in the daylight.

"No, you try so hard to hide this fear you have," she observed. "Last night you made a point of avoiding the knife…"

"I just don't like knives."

"It is deeper; but it does not matter. It makes you no less."

"Nightmares matter, Ku'zn," he whispered, looking directly into her green and amber eyes. "They twist your whole life."

"Dreams can shape a life as well. I hold a dream to return to my island home Z'n Sa with my brother. Someday I will gin my own freedom and purchase him out of contract bondage. Then we will go home to the comforting sea of our own island."

She looked down into T.K.'s eyes and gradually refocused from her dreams to the man curled in her lap. "Some dreams are smaller than others, Grizzlebeard. Sometimes as small as a man."

She bent forward and he reached up to her, twisting his body so that they were in an embrace. Her breath was warm on his cheek. He felt blood rushing to his loins.

"This is no slap in the face, sweetcakes," he whispered, "but as much as I'd like this—and I've been thinking about it since I first saw you—I've got too much male pride to accept this as pity."

Ku'zn's brow knit with a fleeting thought of anger. "Silly male," she whispered, "you're not that pitiful and I'm not that virtuous."

Their lips met and T.K. went warm all over. For a moment there was no pain, no memory, only a connection of two souls who both felt deep need for that connection. Just when they both realized that they might be going too far there was a sudden noise from around the rock.

It was a low throaty sound like a whimper.

Ku'zn sprang upright and T.K. rolled to his knees with his walking stick in hand pulled back into chamber to strike.

The whimper repeated.

The two approached the origin of the sound cautiously, rounding an angle of the rock to see—

"A tvek!" Ku'zn blurted out. "It must have been the family pet."

T.K.'s first encounter with a tvek brought mixed feelings. It was a long-necked, beak-snouted lizard the size of a German shepherd. When the word had come up at the Svora camp Shoutte had explained that while wild tveks were dangerous many Altivans kept tvek as pets and used them to herd svor or to hunt. The iridescent, green-skinned lizards filled the niche dogs and wolves did on Earth in every way with packs of wild tvek much feared in wilderness areas.

This tvek was curled up in a partially dug out hollow beneath the rock, licking several vicious cuts along its flank. It made a deep-throated growl when T.K. approached.

"Be careful," Ku'zn cautioned, "its beak is saber sharp."

"Easy boy," T.K. said in a calming tone. "It's okay, nobody's gonna hurt you." The growl repeated, but the animal made no move.

"He must have tried to fight off the shadowbeast."

"Well," T.K. whispered, "he's the first survivor of a meeting with that thing I know of. The little guy deserves what help we can give him."

"I will bring Erique," Ku'zn said.

"You do that." He put a hand on her arm before she turned away. "And kiddo, I hope that moment back there still has hope to happen."

She touched his cheek with a gentle but strong hand. "In its time, Grizzlebeard. I will like that." He touched her hand and smiled.

"Meanwhile I'll just settle down by this little fellow here and talk to him awhile. And bring my pack too, okay, Peachfuzz?"

✛✛✛

The night was a long one for both T.K. and Shoutte. Each kept a vigil.

Erique sat cross-legged in the doorway of the burning hill house, with Rhythemwand across his lap and chanted in his odd, whispered voice.

T.K. spent the night by the wounded tvek. He bathed and washed the vicious wounds on the beast and put some salve on them that Shoutte gave him. Afterward the warp orphan sketched, read, played his harmonica and talked softly to the wounded creature.

Madame Orancha locked the women in the wagon again and got little sleep, propping herself near the door, grasping a stout cudgel.

In the morning it was red-haired Lunit, wearing her Audrey Hepburn hand-me-down hat, that awakened T.K.

"Oh, hi ducky," T.K. yawned, "How's tricks?"

"The Kovar priest is still by the doorway, mumbling—" Lunit said softly, exchanging a look of mutual suspicion with the tvek, "—and Ku'zn and Orancha have hitched the team."

"It's okay, boy," he said cheerfully to the animal, "she won't bite."

"Oh yes I will," she laughed, "but only if I'm asked."

T.K. rose slowly and then leaned over to pet the tvek softly on the head. It made a sound that started out as a growl but finished as a whimper. "Gotta go boy, but there's water and food for a day or two. You take care now."

The wagon was ready to go when T.K. and Lunit arrived. Ku'zn had saddled Shoutte's mount and pack vorn, and bridled T.K.'s mount.

"Thanks, Peachfuzz."

"Fine thing," Orancha interjected. "My girls working as stable help! No good eunuch!"

"Torval the Eunuch was our stableman," Ku'zn explained. "We lost him to a gambling parlor in Chopanta."

T.K. looked over to see Lord Shoutte still seated cross-legged in the doorway of the farmhouse. Smoke billowed from the house and thick soot covered both Shoutte and the woven blue cloak he wore.

"I'll get Barry Fitzgerald." He walked to the chanting priest and knelt and added in a softer tone. "We're ready to go, Erique."

Lord Shoutte opened his eyes slowly and stared at T.K. for a long moment without recognition. Finally, he took a deep breath and spoke.

"I will conduct you to Tolan," he said in a distant voice, "and aid you to find a wizard. But I will return. Rhythemwand will see this shadowbeast finds its transition. By the Sacred Principle I have sworn it."

Lord Shoutte tossed the blue cloak into the smoky interior. "Let us go."

The two men turned and noticed that the wounded tvek had slunk out to join them. It stood looking indecisively between the hill house and T.K. for a moment, then padded to his side.

"I guess the little fella's adopted me," T.K. said.

"A good companion," Shoutte nodded. "He'll scream a warning of bandits in the night." The tvek eyed the priest curiously.

"Gotta name the little booger then," T.K. murmured. He looked down at the blue-eyed stare from the creature and then laughed with sudden inspiration.

"Since this isn't Kansas, fella," T.K. noted, "you must be Toto." He patted its head. "What do you think Toto, huh?" The tvek nuzzled his hand and the name was set.

"Z'last!" Orancha yelled from her perch on the wagon. She pointed over the hill toward the ocean and repeated, "Z'last!"

T.K. craned his neck but it wasn't until he was mounted that he could see what she was talking about. A massive squall line was visible on the ocean's horizon.

"What is it?" T.K. asked. "It just looks like a heck of a storm."

"'Zlast' is a word from wizard tongue," Shoutte said mounting up. "It is also called a shadowstorm. This whole eastern coast is subject to them."

"Shadowstorm, huh? Bad?"

"Have you noticed the stunted vegetation and twisted trees in this area? It is the reason the farmhouse and barn are underground. Nothing prevails against the Z'last; it can strip the flesh from a full-size man, clear to the bone in minutes with its raging winds."

"Another scenic wonder of Altiva," T.K. muttered. "Just great. What do we do?" He remembered Meegana's words about Roosuf calling the forces of nature—*a shadowstorm against me, she said. This has to be his doing—is he that powerful?*

"Go back or push on," Shoutte replied, "it is a slow-moving storm and we have a full day before it is upon us. The provincial governments maintain safe inns along the coast road, each a day's ride apart from each other and less from here. If we do not lag, we should reach one safely."

"I say push on," Orancha chimed in, "we've wasted enough time talking."

"Like the lady says," T.K. said. "Lead on, MacDuff."

So the group, a warrior priest, a former Marine, one madame and four professional escorts rode southward. And a tvek named Toto, followed.

Chapter Seven

"There is purpose to even the most casual of meetings; every person you meet is there for a reason, even if only to be a doormat."
A Hell's Angel to T.K., just before the fight began.

One of the two vorn T.K. was leading snorted and stumbled amid the increasing howl of the wind, its antlered head bowed against the cutting dirt driven by the storm. The earthman wound the reins around his hands one more time and shouted again, "Where now?"

Lord Shoutte, busy pulling the reluctant lead vorn of the caravan wagon, only motioned to the left with his head in reply.

T.K. veered, his back to the wind, moving through a narrow gap between outcroppings of granite. Shoutte said it had been cut in a winding pattern into baffles to soften the storms' fury. Even so, the earthman did not like their chances of survival in the driving winds unless they reached the inn before the full brunt of the storm was upon them.

At T.K.'s heels, moving with a stubborn head bowed and a distinct limp was the tvek, Toto had refused to ride in the wagon with the women and walked doggedly behind T.K. without a whimper or protest.

T.K. rounded a bend in the path and stopped dead in his tracks.

Looming out ahead of the clouds of dust the wind had caused was the yawning open-mouthed head of some hideous giant beast. The span of its jaws could easily swallow the entire party in one gulp.

T.K. was about to yell "Go back" when an odd fact impressed itself on him; the creature was not moving. Its jaws remained open and still, despite the rising tempest.

The two shining blue eyes stared unblinkingly at him from beneath thick, green-scaled brows. *That's impossible*, he thought. The sand and debris stirred by the wind made it difficult for him to keep his own eyes open beyond a squint and certainly would have blinded even so huge a creature.

"Go!" Shoutte's hoarse whisper pierced the howl beside T.K. He pointed to the looming creature ahead but Shoutte only nodded and croaked, "The inn."

Freakin' weird planet! T. K. thought as he urged the vorn forward.

Within ten steps T.K. realized what Shoutte meant; the reptile's head was sculptured from the living rock of a mountain, its open mouth fitted with two great wooden doors. The doors were fastened with a simple slip latch T.K. threw off easily. Soon the entire caravan was standing beyond the door inside a cavernous stable that was large enough to house four more wagons and teams.

"Damn, that's a mean storm," T.K. commented, spitting dust and wiping sand from his beard and hair. Toto took great delight in rolling in a nearby pile of wet straw to sooth his scarred hide.

"I have never seen a shadowstorm move across the land so fast," Lord Shoutte rasped. "If we had been delayed even a short while I fear we would not have survived."

"It is Keir al saed; an omen of evil," the blue furred Ku'zn said. "A shadow creature has touched this mighty wind."

"Nonsense," Madame Orancha said, "the storm is just a storm." The compact woman was already busy attempting to unharness the vorn from the wagon tongue, but the skittish beasts, annoyed by hours of scathing wind, wouldn't have any of it.

"Curse you for a tvek," Orancha murmured. "Hold still!"

"That no good Torval, my fool helper, went and got his neck broken in the last town for being caught at cheating," Orancha continued. "I'd have broken it myself if we hadn't had to leave in a hurry—oof!" The vorn bucked and the madame landed on her rump with a thud.

"That's it!" she concluded and struggled to her feet with the aid of Lunit, Yomi, and a determined look. "Get away from there, Ku'zn."

"You there," she called, "warp orphan. I can't do this after sitting up there all day; I will make it worth your while to tend to our vorn." T.K. looked at Shoutte. "I could use some local scratch."

"Go ahead," Shoutte approved. "I will finish with Stardancer and meet you in the common room." The priest asked Orancha, "What rate will you pay him?"

"A lin," she answered trying to make it sound magnanimous.

"He works for a brut or you do it yourself," Shoutte stated flatly. T.K. caught the gist of the negotiation and crossed his arms in a 'I'm holding out for overtime' look.

"All right, but he has to feed them too! Let's get cleaned up, girls. Come on." The madam marched off with her troupe of ladies following like a gaggle of goslings.

Shoutte preceded T.K. into the inn by a good half hour, during which the earthman un-harnessed, watered, fed, and quartered the wagon animals in some of the wooden stalls that lined the stone room. It was much the same work as it would have been for any team of horses back in the Dakotas.

The wind howled with increased fury against the outer door.

Toto trotted faithfully behind T.K. matching his steps and accepting an occasional pat on the head and "good boy," from him.

"You know, Toto," T.K. said as he finished hanging the harness tackle, "when all is said and done, shoveling dung is the same everywhere, you know?" The dog-sized lizard looked up with soulful eyes and hissed. T.K. patted his head again.

The earthman shouldered his backpack and smiled down at the lizard. "Let's go see what passes for beer in this funhouse, fella."

+++

Lord Gavilon's war vorn crested the hill with a snort, sensing the drop in air pressure ahead that signaled the approaching z'last. The beast's

"ALL RIGHT, BUT HE HAS TO FEED THEM TOO."

master sensed it too and his bloodless lips parted with annoyance.

"Charm or no charm, we can follow no trail in that," he whispered to his midnight black mount, Thunderblood. "But, should the heir survive, he can make no progress either. We must move ahead of him and await his arrival. Ride hard, Thunderblood, if we miss him, our Lord will peel our souls more completely than this storm could rend our flesh."

He kicked the charger into motion and set off at a trot along the inland road. The road wound through hills, which would shield it from most of the direct shadowstorm's rage. The long loop would place him ahead of his prey, but only if the storm kept the heir pinned down long enough for Gavilon to make the longer inland journey.

It would be a near thing—a gamble.

Long deadened nerves came awake as the bringer of death tingled with the myriad possible deaths that might await him at the Emperor's hands should he fail. It was a sensation, one of the few left to him, that his master often awakened in him and one reason he served the powerful wizard emperor so faithfully.

The Lord Gavilon laughed as he rode and any living thing that heard shuddered in horror.

+++

The inner door of the stable opened into a room of almost equal size. It also was an enlarged natural cave, sloping from just over the earthman's head at the entrance, to three times his height at the opposite end. Stone steps spiraled to a second-floor landing against the far wall, and beneath the landing, a wide stone door led off to what appeared to be a kitchen.

Above the center of the room was a wide skylight, heavily barred to protect the thick glass from wind-hurled debris. Literally snaking down from the skylight was a fireplace flue, carved from some jade-like rock into the shape of a feathered snake. It hung openmouthed above a central fire pit hearth near which Lord Shoutte sat sipping from a crystal mug.

"Ah, Tee-Kay, my friend, I had given you up for lost. Welcome to Dragonthroat." A quick survey of the room revealed only one other person in the room, a solemn, hooded, and masked figure dressed from head to toe in black seated at a far table.

The former marine regarded that ominous figure with a raised eyebrow but when he saw that Shoutte seemed to be relaxed with the mystery figure's presence so he did his best to ignore it.

Maybe it's just a fashion fad, like Goths.

He crossed the space to settle down across the stone table from the priest "That frosty looks good," T.K. said, "Where does one uh—"

Shoutte produced a mug from beside him on the bench. "Here, drink."

"Say no more." T.K. took the proffered mug and sipped. "Not bad," he approved. "To your health." The dark ale disappeared in a single gulp. "That hit the spot, thanks."

"It always restores me to the Rhythem," Shoutte smiled.

"You sure got weird habits for a priest."

"Just enlightened," the Kovar priest said. "Advancing the Kova wherever I can."

Just then a bear of a man, barrel-chested, bald, bearded, and wearing a leather apron, entered the common room from the kitchen, carrying a wooden tray that held several crockery jugs. Toto hissed at him.

"Proprietor!" Shoutte called to the man, "More ale."

The man set one of the jugs down on the table, looked daggers at both men, and moved on to the lone figure in black.

"Real cheerful guy," T.K. remarked as he poured the second round. "What's with The Shadow over there?"

"Not so loud, my warp orphan, friend." Shoutte whispered, "That is a member of the Assassin's Guild."

"Come again?"

"I have had—uh—dealings in the past with guild members, they are formidable enemies," Shoutte continued. "See the knives—" He pointed surreptitiously to two broad bladed forearm length short swords the Assassin wore strapped in crystal sheaths on his forearms. The blade tips poked out past the elbows and the knuckle guard handles protected the back of the hands when sheathed.

"Ruby-Crystal blades," Shoutte said, "grown around drops of the Assassin's blood, like Rhythemwand was grown in drops of mine. It means that he is not one to trouble, despite his small stature."

"These assassin guys—" T.K. asked, "People just let them walk around?"

"They are a registered guild in many countries, though there are those cities and states that will not have them. They are like vipers to those whom they hunt! They kill only on legal warrant or in defense, however and are scrupulous in keeping their word. We really have little to fear. By both royal decree and common law, it is death to fight in anger in a safe inn. While here Pax is observed by all. No violence is allowed at all."

"Reassuring thought," T.K. said, "but who enforces it?"

"The Guild themselves, among other bodies," Shoutte answered. "They would not be tolerated if they were totally unregulated; the nobles of several kingdoms find them valuable. They can pursue criminals across many frontiers, though who exactly is determined to be criminal can make their dedication to justice questionable."

"I guess like bounty hunters back home," T.K. said, "So you've worked with them?"

"They can be dealt with, if one has to. I have, uh… debated successfully with their members, still it is best not to start trouble with them if it can be avoided. They are licensed to kill in many places."

T.K. shivered at the idea of a licensed killer sitting in the same room with him. He realized suddenly that he was staring at the Assassin and, more disturbing, the Assassin was staring back. He smiled and waved.

"Yeah, best to finish the trouble than start it. To reiterate, a charming world, just charming."

The warp orphan regarded the room and the black clad figure, trying hard not to stare at the crystal tips of the knives on the Assassin's arms. Lord Shoutte saw his fascination.

"Yes, those blades are like Rhythemwand," the priest said.

"Like those glow gem things?"

"Not quite," the cleric said. "They do not have the same properties as our crystal weapons. Those glowgems that provide light are also grown so that any light they receive from any source is reflected back for many hours without heat. But can not compare to our blades."

"An amazing world, pal," T.K. said. "I keep finding new reasons to-"

Just then the doors from the stable were flung open and a squat almond-eyed man dressed in torn silk robes entered the room.

"Rise for Her Royal Highness, Tannilee!" Having made his announcement, the little man stepped aside and a brawny giant beneath a steel antlered helmet, dressed in a finely worked leather tunic and carrying a two-handed broadsword as if it were a dagger stepped forward and took in the room at a glance. He glared at the still seated T.K. and Shoutte.

"Arise for the Princess, tveks," he growled, "or feel the wrath of Conkull of Krinaria!"

The earthman and the priest looked lazily at one another and Shoutte nodded yes. Both men rose just as the princess entered the room amid a swirl of colorful silk.

She was coolly beautiful and every inch aware of it. Her ivory-colored hair was worn long and braided with pearls contrasted her skin's red hue.

Her finely chiseled features were just beyond the softness of adolescence and already set in the lines of command—a princess bred, to be sure.

Directly behind her Royal Highness followed an almond-eyed woman, a boy whose silks matched the princess' herald's, and a thin faced, hand-wringing sort of man with the same ruddy skin as the princess. The handwringer spoke first.

"Innkeeper, the princess requires your finest suite," he said in the stentorian tones used to address legions of servants.

"Welcome to Dragonthroat," the innkeeper said from the doorway to the kitchen. "I am Zul, your host, and I am honored by your presence."

"We know," Handwringer said. "You may address us as Lord Rayjol, or your Lordship. You may not address Her Highness."

"Of course, Lord Rayjol," Zul bowed. "Our accommodations are humble, but I and my daughter, we endeavor to..."

"Of course you will," Lord Rayjol said in a bored tone, "Now take us to our quarters, we wish to scrub off the effects of this Z'last. I feel the dirt of the entire kingdom has settled in my clothing."

"Certainly." The burly innkeeper bowed obsequiously.

T.K. had enough. "Hey, what about us?" Shoutte shot a look of horror at T.K. "We're paying customers too!"

The giant guard growled and took a menacing step toward them.

"Excuse me," the priest injected holding up his hand. "May I point out that the laws of hospitality accord us equal rights of lodging and service."

Conkull halted and looked to Lord Rayjol for instruction.

The princess observed everything with a coolly detached eye. The innkeeper stepped between the two groups and, with a glare at T.K. and Shoutte, spoke in a professionally soothing voice, "You will be attended to, my Lord. My daughter will personally see to your accommodations. Zulla!"

At his call, a teenage girl appeared at the door to the kitchen. She had her father's dark coloring, but that was where the resemblance ended. She was slight and elflike, with Kewpie doll eyes that seemed to take in the room from a great distance.

"Yes, Father?" She wore a simple earth brown shift and a too big leather apron, on which she wiped her damp hands.

"Take these good gentles to their rooms, daughter," Zul directed. "After I have shown her Highness' party to theirs." He turned, bowed again to the princess and her party and then led them up the stairs.

"That is a princess of the line, my friend," Shoutte whispered, "One does not cross a princess of the line and live."

T.K. shrugged. "Sorry if I made an Ugly American scene. I just don't like long noses and the people who look down them. It's gotten me kicked out of some the best places from Palo Alto to Phnom Penh."

"Sirs," the young girl said in a tamed voice, "I will show you to your rooms now if you wish." She looked directly at T.K. and smiled. "I am Zulla."

"Well hello, Pumpkin," he smiled back, "I'm T.K. Mitchell."

Toto moved up beside the girl and nosed her leg.

"Tee-kay." She giggled at his smile. "The great poet of Ker Nok was named Tee'Kay; it is an auspicious name."

"I always thought so."

"And I am Lord Erique Shoutte," the priest said. The girl barely noticed he had spoken. Instead she knelt to pet the tvek who accepted her touch with mews and clicks of delight.

"His name is Toto, Pumpkin," the earthman said. "I think he likes you."

"I will take you to your room Tee-kay." The girl led the way up the spiral stairs.

"Shouldn't you keep an eye out for new guests?" T.K. asked.

"No one will come now," she explained. "I am surprised that the princess and her party was able to make it safely. The shadowstorm is here. All the signs are that it will be a bad one too; we could be here a ten-day for this one." She preceded them up the stairs and T.K. followed her lithe form, clearly visible beneath her shift.

"That reminds my sexist mind," T.K. said to the priest, "Where are Orancha's choir girls?"

Shoutte laughed softly. "They are at the mineral pool."

"Pool?"

"A natural hot spring in the inn. We can go there once we have cleaned up."

T.K. smiled. "Well, I can clean up this body, but I'm not going to be able to do much about this mind of mine."

The two men washed in their room with bowls of water provided for that then changed into lounging robes supplied by the inn.

They then made their way to the hot spring down a long corridor from the second floor.

The spring was a vaulted natural space with roughhewn wall with glowgems along the sides and a central pool twenty feet across and five feet deep. The room was already empty of Orancha's ladies and the two men settled into the steaming waters for a singularly pleasant half hour and soaked away the sore hours of trail riding.

Like many men who had spent a warrior life they both were comfortable with silence and enjoyed the bubbling of the spring without words for close to an hour.

"Enough for me my friend," Lord Shoutte, finally said rising from the mineral spring. "Any longer and I shall be fit for garnishing and serving at supper."

The Kovar priest ascended the broad steps out of the small pool, dried off, and wrapped himself in a topaz-colored silk kimono.

T.K. studied the glowgems sconces and could see that when a candle was lit in their center, the clusters, held on a ceramic tray around the candles. The crystals acted as magnifiers of the light, casting a pleasing green-white glow. Shoutte said that when the candle was blown out the glowgems would keep reflecting that light for a long time.

All of the inn that T.K. had seen so far was lit the same way, though the gem-lights varied in hue.

"I'm gonna boil a while longer," T.K. bobbed shoulder deep in the water. "This weird planet is the last place I expected to find a hot tub."

"I will see you in the common room then," Shoutte said, "but don't be too long, the young girl said mid-meal will be served soon and these inns are notorious for cooking too little at each meal so it is first come, first fed."

"Okay, Erique," T.K. sighed, "ten minutes."

With that, the Kovar priest left the warp orphan to himself in the spring room. T.K. eased back into the water and floated on his back.

"I don't believe this, Toto, do you?" The tvek was busily swimming around the pool. From time to time he bumped his head into T.K.'s leg and hissed happily.

"Ah, the voice of wisdom," T.K. said wistfully. "I agree with you, Toto, my lad. I agree." He relaxed for a moment and almost forgot all about the Warps, the deaths, and the ominous wizard emperor who wanted his life.

Almost.

"You. Come out of there. It is time for the princess's bath."

T.K. startled at the shrill voice, sank beneath the surface and came up sputtering.

At the edge of the pool, their travel clothes replaced by radiant silk robes stood the princess and her almond-eyed lady-in-waiting. It was the lady who spoke.

"And take that disgusting beast with you."

Toto, by this time, was hissing at the intrusion of the two women and began to paddle across the pool towards them.

"Keep that thing away from me, Kwa Tzen." The princess spoke with the voice of a ruby statue—quiet, confident, and distant. The attendant hastened to step between her mistress and the approaching tvek.

"Ease up, your highness," T.K. said. "You just startled us. Here, Toto." He reached out and patted the animal on the rump, which caused it to veer off from its target and paddle in a wide circle back toward him.

"Regardless, you will leave now," the attendant repearted. She so expected compliance that she turned her back and began to help her mistress disrobe.

"There's plenty of room," T.K. pulled Toto to his side and floated to the opposite side of the pool from the women. "Neither one of us bites unless asked and with the rules of equal hospitality and all..." he said as the thought occurred to him, smiling at them. *This isn't Malibu; who the hell knows what a man and woman in the same tub means here—I might be asking her to marry me. Poor thing if she accepts!*

But the damage, if any, had been done. The princess, with a child's laugh, flung off her robe. She stood naked on the edge of the pool for a moment, flaunting her newly realized womanly form, pretending to wait impatiently for Kwa Tzen to remove her own clothing. Neither woman showed the least embarrassment at their nudity.

T.K. made no attempt to hide his artist's appreciation of the princess' red-bronze body or his delight in the fact that her pubic and underarm hair matched the ivory of her scalp. Toto, delighted to have his neck scratched, hissed at almost a purr.

"The water temperature is wonderful, Your Highness," Kwa Tzen said as she descended the steps into the water. The princess seemed to concur, her icy manner melting as she felt the warmth of the spring water rise around her.

"You can feel the water swirling below," she giggled in a very unregal manner. "It tickles."

"That's the water inlet," T.K. said. "The spring bubbles up from the bottom and runs off through those little holes on the side." He pointed and the princess nodded.

"From whence do you come, sirrah?" Tannilee asked after a few moments of soaking.

"A place called Palo Alto."

"Where is that?" the princess asked. "Surely nowhere in my father's realm." The earthman laughed.

"Far from it, hon. Lord Shoutte called me a warp orphan." The young woman's expression lit up at that.

"You are a warp orphan? You have been through a warp portal?" she asked.

"That's how I got here. Just another unexpected side trip to my life."

"I have yet to be allowed through a portal," the princess confessed. "My father said that he does not trust warp wizards and says they might send me anywhere."

"I'm getting the impression that warp wizards are not a popular group of people."

Kwa Tzen watched the exchange with disdainful eyes, which were always conscious of Toto, who was once again paddling free.

"What's it like?" Tannilee asked eagerly. "I have wanted to go though one for so long. It seems like fun."

"I don't really remember," T.K. replied. "I wasn't really myself at the time."

"Oh, who were you?" the princess asked with great interest.

T.K. just smiled and looked to heaven for an answer. "It's a long story. I'll tell you another time, but whoever I was, he was a better guy."

The royal teenager lay back in the pool and let her hair trail out behind her in the water. "Sing for me Kwa Tzen," she commanded. The lady in waiting nodded.

"Yes, your Highness," she said, "What should I sing?"

"Sing a festival song. The Beseecher's Song."

"Very well, Highness," the servant woman said and, with hesitation, added, "But is that really a suitable song for your ears? It's rather common"—Kwa Tzen blushed——"almost improper."

T.K. burst out laughing. "Let's hear it for impropriety!"

"Are you always so insolent?" Tannilee asked.

He thought for a moment, and then nodded. "Yup. Got a string of classic black eyes to prove it."

The lady in waiting took a deep breath and then began to sing in a clear, mature voice:

"*Will her eyes be green or blue,*
Will his smile be crooked too
Will his soul be scarred by countless thoughtless fools
And his tears have formed a myriad of pools?
Will he hum or sing or giggle

In the showers,"

T.K. watched the young royal who, like any teenage girl, let a wistful smile flash across her lips. She leaned her head back as the maid sang to her. Her white hair floated out behind her like a mass of seaweed. When the girl noticed the earthman watching her she even lowered her guard enough to give him a half smile and blush a bit and give him a half smile.

"Will he see my pain and soothe me by the hour?

Delicate or raw, Dark or fair

Just as long as a soul is there—

Funny, noble, kind and strong,

Like a hero from a bardic song.

Oh Gods who rule above,

This is my prayer

To find my love..."

Suddenly Kwa Tzen squealed and attempted to leap straight out of the water. She landed with a splash, running for the side of the pool. "The monster!" was all she screamed in explanation, but it was enough when Toto surfaced with what looked like a satisfied smile right where the woman had been standing.

"Oh, Toto," T.K. groaned, "Do as I say, not as I do!" The earthman snatched up the tvek and headed out of the pool.

"'Scuse me ladies, I hear my mother calling me to dinner." Still naked, T.K. snatched up his robe and headed out into the hall. Behind him Kwa Tzen launched a string of invectives that would peel the paint off a battleship and make a sailor blush while Tannilee roared with regal laughter.

+++

Mid-meal was the main meal on Altiva, served about an hour after the larger, slower sun had set. T.K. decided to dress for the occasion and so put on his 'newish' pair of blue jeans and a green T-shirt with a full color Mickey Mouse drawing on the front. He completed the ensemble with a diaphanous, multi-colored silk scarf as a headband, given to him by a stripper in Des Moines, Iowa. On Toto he fastened a rhinestone dog collar given to him by the self-same stripper.

"Come on, boy," he said inspecting the two of them in a looking crystal, "Let's show the yokels how it's done." Toto hissed in agreement.

The common hall was almost full when T.K. arrived.

The princess and her party were seated at two of the rectangular tables set end-to-end dead center in the room.

Madame Orancha's brood was dressed to kill in elegant silks and bangles that were more suggestions than clothes and had occupied one of the round tables off to one side. They waved and giggled like schoolgirls when T.K. entered. He waved back and almost collided with the young girl Zulla, who was carrying a tray of food almost her size.

"Here, Pumpkin," he offered. "Let me help you with that."

"No, it's alright," the girl said, but as she said it she all but tripped on a rough spot in the floor. T.K. intercepted the tray just as she caught her balance.

"Thank you," breathed even as her cheeks colored pink.

He helped her carry the tray to a serving station at the hearth where she set about distributing dishes. "If father saw me talking to you, he would punish me."

"Here in front of all these people?"

"He can get very angry."

"Just as long as he doesn't want any svor," T.K. said. When the girl looked at him oddly, he just smiled. "Do you and your father run the whole inn all by yourselves, Pumpkin?"

Zulla nodded. "But it is not always so busy. Mostly we just tend to the fungus farm in the old mine that is beneath the inn. We even make enough extra to sell to traveling peddlers for extra supplies."

"Must be lonely for a pretty little girl like you."

"Do you really think I'm pretty?" she asked. T.K. nodded and she blushed. "I don't mind the loneliness most times, I have my drawings to keep me company."

"I draw too, honey. I'd like to see yours." He suddenly found himself amused by the sound of what he was saying. "I'll show you some of mine."

Oh My God—did I just say I'll show you mine if you show me yours to a kid? I need a beer.

The child beamed. "Oh yes, I would like that. Sometimes I draw people who pass through here and then I talk to the drawings sometimes when I get real lonely. Or..." her expression grew troubled. "Or when I have nightmares sometimes."

T.K. chucked her under the chin and nodded, "I can understand that, Kidstuff. I get lonely too, sometimes and I know too much about nightmares."

"Zulla, come here. Help me, girl!" The voice of the girl's father boomed out of the kitchen and she almost jumped into the fire pit.

"Yes, father," she called back, "I am coming." She whispered, "I must go," and raced off before T.K. could react.

He shrugged and, palming a biscuit from the serving tray, walked over to where Shoutte sat by himself at a table near Orancha's brood. The priest was shaking his head and clucking.

"Let her go, my friend," Shoutte advised. T.K. looked at him questioningly. "She's young, she'll meet some peddler or svorherd who'll sweep her off her feet and she'll settle down in some thatched cottage." He offered T.K. a tankard of ale as the earthman sat on a bench at the table.

"I could settle down with the right lady," the earthman said. "Though not somebody that young, for sure. But she's sweet and I just can't stand to see lives wasted, ya know?"

"Though you try to hide it, my friend," Shoutte whispered. "You are a warrior and a wanderer. We have nothing but ourselves to offer. It is a gift of short duration for any who accept it."

"I'm no warrior," T.K. argued. "Not anymore. But I suppose you're right. It's just that she looks so helpless, so frail." He shook his head and took a swig of the drink.

A voice nearby said, "So you like them helpless, huh?" It was the blue furred Ku'zn, who had been passing their table with a tray of bread. T.K. and Shoutte both burst out laughing. She tried her best to look docile and helpless, but her muscular body and the scars visible beneath her fur on her sword arm worked against her.

"Anytime you need a hangnail taken care of," T.K. said, "or the pickle jar opened, give me a call, Peachfuzz."

"Ku'zn, stop that," Orancha called. "I won't have you wasting energy on non-paying customers." The Z'n woman cast her employer a look that should have killed, but it was coco-skinned Adriana who spoke next.

"You can't control our free time here," she said. "It is intus pax."

"Like Krost I can't!" Orancha fumed. "Your contracts to me state..."

"Beg pardon, Madame Orancha," the tiny Yomi said, "but, by hostelry law, all contracts, kanely and civil law, are suspended while within these walls."

"You can't..." fumed the older woman.

"We most certainly can," the red haired Lunit said with the glee of a schoolchild correcting the teacher. "Only the hostelry law of pax is valid— no hand may be raised in anger. All other laws, arguments and contracts are suspended while we are confined."

Orancha looked fit to be tied, but it was an argument she had lost before, if with less finality. She turned back to her ale and guzzled down a double serving.

The women looked pleased and all turned their attention toward Lord Shoutte and T.K. The earthman and the priest looked at one another with the sudden pleasant realization that they were the real issue in the argument and that the side of liberation had won.

T.K. grinned. "Gonna be an interesting couple of days."

+++

"How the hell are we supposed to track them in this?" The bandit called Sword wrapped his scarf more tightly around his neck in a vain effort to hold out some of the swirling dust the storm pushed before it. "It's insane," he continued, "or do you have powers to go with your wizard charms? Can you fly?"

"It's pretty clear they're heading for Tolan," the massive, bald Axe said. "We just have to follow the road."

"What road?" Sword yelled. "The only thing clear is that you're crazy." He waved his arms with fury almost equal to the storm. "That is a Z'last blowing up. It'll strip our skin to the bone. It's a shadowstorm, man, or are you not smart enough to realize that? We will die!"

The acrid smoke from the still smoldering hill farmhouse surrounded the eight men standing near the corral and made the already darkening afternoon sky black. It matched the mood of the group.

"This charm does have power," Axe said clutching the serpent necklace that Roosuf's winged messenger had brought him. It will protect us through even a Z'last."

"Says who?" Sword demanded.

Axe leaned forward, an old scar along his left temple throbbing white and whispered, "You doubt the word of the Wizard Roosuf?"

Sword reacted to the question the way Axe had hoped he would. He was stunned. One did not speak ill of a warp wizard, the dreaded Roosuf least of all without fear of dreaded consequences.

The six other men in the pack watched closely, as jackals watch two lions locked in a death struggle. Only the strongest would survive any confrontation and it was as it should be: these men would follow only the strongest.

"It—it's still madness to go into one of those." The two men never broke eye contact as Sword spoke. "I won't do it."

Axe grinned, a hideous, self-assured grin that showed a line of rotten twisted teeth that resembled fangs.

"You either go with us," he said quietly, "or you stay here permanently. I want those two sons of a tvek. No one gets away from me, ever." He let the words hang in the air, then stepped away from Sword and turned his back.

The wiry Sword reacted immediately; drawing his sword to slice at Axe's back almost faster than the eye could follow.

Much faster, though, was Mace, a stocky troll of a man whose namesake weapon crushed the back of Sword's head before the blade's arc was complete.

Axe, meanwhile, had turned; ready to parry the cut that never completed. He watched the other six descend on the corpse and strip it of all valuables with a practiced indifference. When they were finished, they looked to him and he nodded.

Then he jogged off down the road into the heart of the shadowstorm showing no fear.

The others, like wolves scenting blood, obediently followed.

Chapter Eight

"I've never met anyone half as smart as you are; nothing alive could be that stupid."
T.K. Mitchell to a Shore Patrol officer, just before the fight.

The midmeal was served in four courses: soup, sweetmeats and bread, a main dish of barley and meat (which to T.K. looked and tasted distinctly turkey-like), and fruit pies for desert as well as liberal supplies of wine and ale. Perhaps because of the presence of the princess there was more than enough food for everyone.

The black-garbed assassin ate alone with cold, appraising eyes that always seemed to focus in the direction of T.K. and Lord Shoutte's table. There were also two new occupants of the room, a rotund, squint-eyed man, and a thin ferret of a man. Jonzun and his crony, Olzen.

"Have you noticed our two new traveling companions?" Lord Shoutte asked of the earthman.

T.K. recognized the bandits immediately. "The two knuckleheads from the wagon." He started to rise but a whispered laugh from Shoutte halted him.

"No need for haste, my friend," the priest said, "Intus Pax is in effect. They can go nowhere until the storm is over and should you raise your hand against them, the penalties will be severe." T.K. shrugged and sat down just as the four women at a near table burst into laughter.

"But that's not all," Orancha was saying, "then he asked for my blessing!" Gales of laughter came from her ladies again.

"Will you give me your blessing later, priest?" The plump and sensual red headed Lunit asked Shoutte with a melodious giggle.

"Why, dear one," the priest whispered in reply, "a priest of the Law of Eternal Change is always ready to bless a true believer." His eyes twinkled with humor as he spoke in a serious tone. It was hard for T.K. to be sure if he was serious or executing a double entendre.

"I know all about you Kovar priests," Lunit said. "I worked in a church contract house for a year; it was very instructive." She smiled.

"Church contract house?" T.K. asked, half expecting the answer he got.

"We of the Kova do not have life marriages like many other religions," Shoutte began. He spoke with the quiet excitement of the convinced. "We have term contracts. Of course, many choose a life partner, but as a way of reaffirming the partnership this must be done in a series of one-year contracts." The priest paused, both for dramatic effect and to down another mug of ale.

"No two contracts may be consecutive with the same partner," Shoutte continued, "so partners may contract for a single hour or night with someone else at one of our Kovar run contract houses. Then they may re-contract for a year. Of course, one is not required to consummate such a contract, but the option is there. Thus Kovar marriages are the most faithful of any I know of."

"Some of the churches on my world, in a more enlightened time, had those sorts of annexes," T.K. said, "Complete with their own vestal virgins."

"Oh, there are no virgins in these houses," Shoutte said. "That is too important a transition. No, sisters and brothers of the Order Kova Nasta, a lay religious order, serve there. Occasionally professionals like Lunit are employed in busy times or when there are not enough brothers and sisters of the order available. The practice truly makes for fidelity during the contract term and provides funds for the indigent out of the church coffers as well."

"Seems like a very civilized practice," T.K. said.

"We think so," Erique said with a satisfied smile.

"But what about V.D?" T.K. asked. Shoutte looked at him with a total lack of understanding, so the earthman elaborated. "You know, venereal disease."

"WILL YOU GIVE ME YOUR BLESSING LATER, PRIEST?"

"I am sorry, my friend," the priest said, "perhaps the linguarings are not translating the idioms correctly, but I do not understand your meaning." The women who were listening with rapt attention had the same puzzled expressions on their faces.

"Okay," the earthman said, "disease transmitted by sexual contact."

"Oh, lice!" Shoutte laughed, "Anyone with any sense can avoid them."

"No, no," T.K. shook his head. "Sunday Morning Surprise, the Clap. Cooties. Syphilis. Gonorrhea, AIDS—You know, stuff you get from sheep and monkeys."

"Who is Sheep?" Shoutte asked, totally lost.

"Moonkee?" Ku'zn said with great curiosity.

Of course, T.K. thought, *I haven't seen a single wool item and they herd lizards. Who would want to make it with one of them ugly things?* He looked down at faithful Toto sitting at his side and patted the tvek on the head. No offense fella.

"Forget it," the earthman said aloud, "just a reoccurring nightmare of mine."

"Such a grim subject," Lunit interjected. "Why dwell on absurd possibilities?"

"Yes," Ku'zn agreed, "I like you two better when you make music than when you talk, I think." T.K. was about to quip at the women in defense when a roar from the royal's table silenced the whole room.

"Service!" The barbarian Conkull bellowed, pounding on the table. "The Princess of Cosen requires service!" Zulla raced from the kitchen with her harried father appearing in the doorway behind her.

"Yes, your lordship," the teenager said quietly. She brushed back a lock of hair that had escaped from the wimple she wore while cooking and kept her gaze lowered in proper reverence.

"Clear the table," the chamberlain Rayjol said as he placed his napkin on his plate. When Zulla hurried to comply he added, "The princess first, you bumpkin!"

Zulla bowed and moved quickly to Her Royal Highness and began to clear the huge porcelain platters from the table.

"Hurry up, girl," Rayjol prompted as the teen raced back from the kitchen to finish the clearing. "Watch that you don't spill any." She frantically tried to comply, but in doing so she moved too fast and splashed some gravy from one of the plates onto Rayjol's sleeve.

"You clumsy whelp!" Lord Rayjol shot upright with such speed that he startled Zulla into dropping most of the plates she was carrying. This of course, aside from the terrible clatter, caused more of the gravy to splash onto the hem of Lord Rayjol's embroidered robe.

Conditioned by a life among servants, he slapped Zulla across the face without a second thought. Zulla, more stunned than hurt, dropped what remained of the plates she was holding and began to cry soundlessly.

Lord Rayjol looked down at his robes and, seeing the damage the gravy had actually done, drew his hand back with very deliberate thought to strike the terrified girl again.

"Touch her again, hairbag," T.K. said in a deadly calm voice that filled the cavernous room, "and I'll break off the arm that does it."

The entire assembly in the room gasped as one and turned to stare at the earthman.

T.K. stood slowly and stared directly into Lord Rayjol's eyes as if to clear up any doubt as to who had spoken. Toto stood beside his new master and hissed in bestial solidarity.

Lord Shoutte, as stunned as anyone else by the earthman's rash defiance, recovered quickly and rose to stand beside his friend. "I am The Reverend Lord Erique, Shoutte of Shoutte in Umbria, your Lordship. What my rash friend means to say is that surely the girl has been sufficiently punished for her minor offense with a single reprimand."

"I mean no such thing." T.K. insisted his focus, darting between the arrogant eyes of the chamberlain and the tear-swollen eyes of the teenager. His rage grew. "The bastard should have his face rearranged for touching her."

The eyes of everyone in the room widened with shock at the sheer audacity of the earthman's pronouncement. Zulla's swollen eyes reflected more than shock as she watched her hero stand up for her; it was a look her father watched with growing concern.

"Will you be quiet?" Lord Shoutte whispered to T.K., "or are you trying to commit suicide?" Shoutte tried to bodily force the earthman to sit but the damage was done; Conkull had risen and started around the table toward T.K.

"Take heed, sirrah!" Lord Shoutte cautioned the barbarian. "It is Pax within these walls—it is death to draw in anger!"

The giant swordsman hesitated a moment and then looked to Lord Rayjol for instruction. It was Princess Tannilee who spoke, however, in a quiet regal tone. The words she spoke words chilled the room more than T.K.'s outburst had.

"Pay no heed to the priest, Conkull," she said. "You draw on royal command to... instruct the warp orphan in the Khonall—the sword dance." She looked contemptuously at T.K. and added, "If an accident were to occur such as the loss of the limb he threatened to strike our Chamberlain with... Well, one cannot account for the whims of the Goddess Yulin." The barbarian nodded respectfully to the Princess and then chuckled fiendishly as he slowly drew his sword.

"Now you're done," Lord Shoutte whispered to T.K. "Here, take Rhythemwand." He edged around to offer the blade to the earthman. T.K. looked at the blade and shook his head.

"I appreciate the gesture," T.K. said with his eyes locked with Conkull's, "it being tuned to you and all, Erique, but no thanks."

The earthman picked up a wood and metal bound tankard in his right hand and what looked very much like a turkey leg in his left. "These are all I need to take care of King Kong."

Conkull strode out into the middle of the room and growled at the earthman. "Pick up a sword, warp orphan, or I shall carve you like a fatted svor. Be a man and give me a contest."

T.K.'s eyes narrowed. "You don't have to carry a butcher's knife to be a man, hairbag. You shouldn't even have to fight." He caught himself taking the fight seriously and shot a glance over to the worried Zulla. He growled in imitation of Conkull for comic effect to get a faint smile from her.

The men circled as they spoke.

"Steel and crystal are the measures of a man," Conkull said, as he lovingly caressed the pommel of his broadsword. "Steel and crystal rule."

T.K. laughed a haunted laugh. "Flesh and bone are what it's all about, muscle mind!" He smiled a humorless smile at the barbarian.

"If this is gonna be a dance lesson, we ought to have some music," T.K. said aloud to the room. "Hey, Peachfuzz," he called to Ku'zn who was, along with everyone else, watching the impending bloodshed with both excitement and horror. "How about playing something lively for me and Steroids here. I'd prefer the 'Stones' but I'll take anything I can *Bossa Nova* to."

The blue-furred woman took a moment to think her way through the earthman's idioms and then laughed. She produced her *Sar Natta*, her Z'n bagpipe made from the heart of a sea worm. It had carved wooden playing pipes which looked like frozen tentacles. She filled her lungs with a massive inhalation of air and then the shrieking tune began, and so did the fight!

The enraged and insulted Conkull could stand no more and he charged the earthman, swinging his great sword in an arc which would have halved T.K. had it connected.

Fortunately, it did not.

T.K. hopped back as if in a comic jig so that the blade tip missed his chest by mere inches. Then as the point passed him, carried inexorably to the conclusion of its arc by inertia, T.K. darted in and smacked the barbarian in the side of the head with the 'turkey' leg.

Conkull roared with indignation and brought his sword back to strike for the earthman. T.K. dropped below the blade's arc and then popped upright, striking with the mug to Conkull's elbow and the turkey leg to the other side of his head.

Conkull jumped back with a squeal of pain and clutched at his numb elbow, ignoring the meat juice dripping down his face.

The rest of the patrons (save for those at the royal party's table) were convulsed with laughter at the giant's befuddlement.

Even Ku'zn had trouble playing the *Sar Natta* as part of her wind went into a stifled chuckle. Nonetheless the jig music continued and T.K. kept step with it.

As fast and as agile the barbarian was (for he was by no means a buffoon with the sword) he was no match for the *arnis*-style training of the earthman. For every arc or thrust he could make with the broadsword, T.K. parried with the tankard and struck a humiliating blow with the turkey leg, literally dancing rings about the muscular bodyguard.

Finally, T.K. made a glancing parry with the turkey leg and crashed the edge of the tankard into the back of Conkull's hand with enough force to disarm him. Before the giant's howl of pain had concluded T.K. stepped back and executed a perfect spinning heel kick so that his right foot slammed into the side of Conkull's head with a resounding thwack not unlike a two-by-four being broken over a brick wall.

The barbarian tottered a moment, his eyes glazed over and his face slack, then he pitched forward to the floor, unconscious.

The music stopped and the room exploded into cheers of delight—cheers which were stilled abruptly when the earthman turned to focus his eyes on Tannilee and then purposely strode across the room to stand directly in front of her.

The universe narrowed to the two of them for a while and none in the room was sure what would come next. Everyone seemed to hold their breath.

Would he hit her?

Would she hit him?

The princess slowly stood up, her eyes locked with T.K.'s, her swelling bosom pressed against Mickey Mouse's belly on his t-shirt. She held up a royal hand to stay Rayjol's attempt to get between her and T.K. and dared the earthman with her gaze.

"Your monkey fell down, lady," he said in a tense whisper. "Pick'em up and send him to dance class, he's got no stamina and he hit my foot with his head."

She glared at him for moment longer and then exploded toward the stairs as fast as her legs could carry her. The royal party followed, save for Rayjol who halted to assist the now groggy Conkull to his feet.

"By Kron and Milthra!" the giant began, but was stopped by Rayjol.

"Oh shut up, you oaf," the chamberlain hissed, "to think I raised you as my own. Come along." He half pushed, half dragged the barbarian up the stairs, followed by a new barrage of laughter.

"I do not know how to repay you, sir," Zulla said to T.K. He tried not to notice her adoring eyes.

"Don't mention it, Pumpkin. I would've done it sooner or later; I can't stand top brass types." He smiled distractedly. "And call me T.K., I'm really not a sir type."

"As you wish, Tee-Kay." The girl looked as if she were about to say something more but choked herself to silence when her father appeared at the earthman's elbow.

"Well fought, sir," the innkeeper said. "Have an ale." He replaced T.K.'s empty scarred tankard with a full one. "I am going to hang this on the wall once the high ones have left." He said, and then added, "There's an epic song to come out of this night." His exuberance went so far that have the innkeeper gave the earthman a hearty slap on the back before he shooed his daughter into the kitchen to prepare a celebration.

T.K. took a deep draught of the ale before rejoining Lord Shoutte at their table.

"Truly foolish, my friend," Shoutte said, "but truly inspiring." He laughed his strange, whispered laugh and joined T.K. in a tankard-draining toast.

"To stupidity," T.K. toasted, "of which I am blessed in abundance."

"And stamina," Adrianna spoke from beside them.

"You are a magnificent warrior," Ku'zn bubbled. "You must teach me that style of fighting."

"I'm not a warrior; I'm just a former leatherneck who lost my cool, that's all," the earthman insisted. He poured a fresh drink from the jug on the table and attempted to dive into it, but the delicate voice of Yomi stopped him.

"No, you fought without heat." The little woman said. "You saved the heat for your words with the princess, where it could be safely vented." She smiled shyly. "You have self control. That bodes well in a man."

"Yes, I like a man with control," Ku'zn said.

"They last longer," Lunit concluded.

Lord Shoutte and T.K. exchanged a conspiratorial smile that conveniently buried T.K.'s embarrassment at the violence.

"A man should not be greedy," Shoutte said piously as he accepted Yomi on his lap for a hug. "He should know his limitations."

"If I find mine," T.K. said, "I'll write them down." T.K. shivered as Ku'zn ran her fingers up his neck and Adrianna leaned over to pour him another drink.

Lunit was persuaded to start the celebration with a song and she smiled at Lord Shoutte and said, "I will sing this one for you, Sir Priest of the Crystalsword.

Sword of my soul, Edge of my heart, Blade of religion, Sharp from the start, Sing of my hope, A song of tomorrow, Hymn of remembrance, Love, pain and sorrow, Cut through the shadows, Of death all to come, 'til victory sheathes you, and my life's work is done."

The Kovar priest was so touched by the song than he bowed to the red-haired siren and touched the knuckles of her hand to his forehead. "You sing like a soul set free," he praised. "I wish I could pay you in kind."

"Oh, I'll think of something that will be of equal value," she suggested with a lascivious grin.

The song began an evening at the inn that, while not a late one, was boisterous. Ale and even some wine flowed freely. T.K, Erique, the four women, the two thieves (who proved to be companionable drinking partners), Zul, and even Orancha joined in the merriment, which consisted of bawdy songs, drinking challenges, and dancing to flute, *Sar Natta* and harmonica music.

Young Zulla retired early at her father's polite but stern insistence, but not before T.K. treated her to an impromptu lesson in some of the Frugge and the Watusi. Zul was not amused.

Through it all, no member of Tannilee's party stirred from their suite.

The entire evening, the Assassin sat silent off to one side at a table by themself and, for all appearances, was lifeless and unmoving save for eyes that missed nothing.

The conviviality eventually ran its course and the weariness of the hard travel to the inn won. Everyone retired, their spirits floating on a cloud of liqueur.

Jonzun and his crony Olzen staggered up to their room unescorted. Meanwhile T.K. was happily accompanied by the blue-furred Ku'zn and dark-skinned Adrianna.

Lord Shoutte surrendered himself to the gentle arms of Lunit and Little Yomi while even the inebriated Orancha consoled herself in the muscular arms of Zul after he attended to securing the inn.

No one noticed when the Assassin left the room, but the black clad figure was gone before the revelers disbursed, presumably gone to their own room.

Outside the Z'last's fierce winds punished the countryside with unrelenting fury, slashing the surface of the land with a million razor-edged grains of sand. The scream of the storm pounded against the crystal roof of the inn like a waterfall.

Inside the pounding fury was one of passion. T.K. lost himself first in the muscular warmth of Ku'zn (a sensation unlike any of his lexicon of his amorous experiences) and then in the sinewy eroticism of the ebony Adrianna. Eventually the inner storms passed and a sated exhaustion settled over the entire inn.

Almost.

"You presumptuous creature," Tannilee screamed at her attendant Kwa Chun. "To criticize our decision." The servant cowered away from the enraged princess while the woman's husband and son watched, unable to interfere.

"Your highness, I did not mean to imply that either dress was not becoming—"

"Now you contradict us!" the princess shrieked.

"But Highness—" Kwa Chun began one last time, but was cut short when the princess rushed forward as if to strike her.

Suddenly Lord Rayjol, who had viewed the whole incident from across the apartment, stepped between them.

"If I might suggest a solution, Highness—" He began, only to feel the sting of Tannilee's slap across his right cheek. Her handprint was soon clearly visible on his face, outlined in bright red.

"And now you dare to oppose our will!" the royal daughter screamed. She was so angry that she actually stamped her feet and shook her fist in the air.

"Only your willfulness," Rayjol whispered through clenched teeth. His eyes were jade beacons whose incandescent glow was dampened by the sharp mind that controlled them. He smiled diplomatically. "You must remember the unusual circumstances which lead to our being here, Highness." Rayjol said in a subdued tone. "His Most Majesty, Shaldulee, your father, would be—"

"Enough," the princess said in a suddenly terrified tone. "Deal with it," she said with finality and vanished into her chambers.

The Chamberlain turned his attention to the Kwa family. "We must realize that her highness Tannilee has not been herself since this... incident began and make allowances," he said in a conciliatory tone. "As the prophet said, 'Great patience brings great rewards.' Understood?"

"Yes, Lord Rayjol," the woman bowed. "It is as you said, the princess has not been herself."

Rayjol nodded. "Fetch both dresses," he said. "In the morning she will be thinking more clearly, and no doubt agree with your fine assessment of the garment." He made a small nod of dismissal and then went into the inner chamber.

"Are you well, wife?" Kwa Tzen whispered, holding Kwa Chun's hand. The woman nodded.

"Not herself," she sneered, "she's been mad since this running began."

"I wanted to hit him when he hit you, mother," their son Kwa Tan said, hugging his mother's waist. The woman smiled at him and patted him on the head.

"It is good you didn't my son, for wrong or right, such as she rules the rest of us."

Moments later the maidservant was in the hall. "Royal bitch!" she whispered as she hurried down the damp chill corridor on her way to the stable to retrieve the dresses from the baggage train.

The injured servant never noticed the portion of the shadows that stepped free into the dim light of the glow gems when the maid passed.

The shadow listened until Kwa Chun's steps were distant and descending the spiral stairs then it moved down the corridor searching. At the door to Lord Shoutte's room the shadow halted. A black-gloved hand caressed the door bolt and the ovar wood door slowly opened.

Inside the glowgems had been night veiled, their blue light streamed into the corridor, and the shadow resolved itself into the shape of the Assassin.

The Assassin entered the room with noiseless steps but kept hollowed against the rough-hewn stone of the wall. Lord Shoutte lay nude on his back in the center of the circular sleep platform, the tiny form of Yomi huddled in a ball beneath his left arm, and the red haired Lunit lying off to one side wrapped in stolen bedclothes.

Yomi's outthrust arm and the top of a sheet framed the Omphast brand on the priest's chest. The Assassin's eye fixed on the brand, the perfect spot through which to thrust the ruby crystal blade held in their hand.

With one hand the Assassin drew off the black cowl, freeing her white gold hair from a topknot while the other hand brandished a blade and prepared to kill the Kovar priest.

In the exultation of the moment, she failed to notice the change in Lord Shoutte's breathing or the minute flexing of the muscles in his sword arm which lay less than half a meter from the sheathed Rhythemwand.

✦✦✦

T.K. was in the nightmare again. He knew now it was The nightmare but as always it was so real that he could not will himself out of it. He could feel the humid heat of the jungle air pressing in all around him. He twitched and moaned, trying to fight his way out of the enhanced reality of the dream state but the jungle refused to go—the verdant, virulent, infectious jungle engulfed him with its suffocating and fetid life.

Green. Brilliant green and haunting.

Then suddenly it was turned crimson by a high-pitched scream.

T.K. was suddenly awake again and puzzled, because the scream was not the usual one he heard in the dream.

Then he heard it again and realized it was not in his head; it was coming from somewhere in the inn!

Chapter Nine

"Paranoia is its own reward."
T.K. Mitchell

Kwa Chun walked through the deserted main room of Dragonthroat with unnatural stealth. Despite the tortured howling of the storm against the great skylight in the room there was a tomb-like silence about the place that compelled her to almost tip toe as she moved. She hurried her steps, anxious to get back to the comforting noise of the royal suite.

Eighteen years old, the woman thought acidly, *and never a more spoiled and willful child have I seen*. She clucked out loud and startled herself with the over importance the sound had in the cavernous main room. She then chided herself for her fear as 'silly' and moved on.

Kwa Chun opened the double doors to the stable and recoiled immediately from the increased howl of the storm and chilled darkness that roiled out at her from the room.

"Fool that I am," she yelled at herself aloud, as if daring the darkness, "I should have brought a lantern, the glowgems are all night veiled."

She groped her way slowly in the almost total darkness, ignoring the nervous bleating of the vorns and the swirl of dust that the drafts from the big room had stirred up. She found the royal wagon and was climbing the steps into it when the vorns' nervous bleating became frightened squeals. Suddenly she knew she was not alone in the stable.

"Who is there?" Kwa Chun called out, an annoyed tone masking her fear. "Speak up. I will have no skulking about." She strained her eyes against the darkness, trying to decipher the shadows. "Is that you, husband, come to whimper at me again to forgive you? If you have, forget it."

The vorns were now frantic, snorting and kicking their stalls, creating a din that all but drowned out the Z'last. It was so loud it kept Kwa Chun from hearing the growl from behind and above her on the wagon's roof.

But no sound, not even the Z'last, could muffle the scream of terror and pain from Kwa Chun when something leapt on her back from the top of the wagon.

✦✦✦

In his room Erique Shoutte bolted upright at the scream, Rhythemwand in hand. His eyes were focused on the vacant doorway. *I'll deal with you later, friend*, Shoutte thought. He threw on a robe while keeping an eye on the doorway and a hand near his sword.

"Was that a scream?" Yomi asked sleepily, but the warrior-priest was already out of the room and in the corridor.

Shoutte almost collided with Toto and a limping T.K., who wore only his blue jeans and carried his ankle brace and walking stick. Ku'zn rumple-furred and naked, stood beside the earthman holding a jeweled dirk. The three exchanged questioning looks.

"That way, I think," Shoutte whispered indicating the direction of the common room.

The three turned as one and raced down the corridor with a groggy, Toto limping behind. Behind them heads were poking out of rooms to see what the commotion was.

Shoutte was the first onto the landing above the main room but the room already had one occupant; the assassin stood by the open door to the stable like a shrouded messenger of death. There were glowgems that had been unveiled so that the figure stood stark black in the brighter room.

"There is no hurry," the cowled figure said quietly, "The woman is quite dead." The trio descended the stairs at a cautious pace, senses alert for some sort of trick. Toto hissed noncommittally and eyed the black clad Assassin suspiciously. Shoutte kept his focus on the Assassin.

"Who's dead, Lamont?" T.K. asked as he approached.

In answer, the woman swung open the stable doors all the way so that a finger of light pointed into the darker room and illuminated the gory remains of Kwa Chun.

"Oh, hell in a hand basket!" T.K turned away from the sight just in time to see the woman's son at the foot of the stairs, ahead of the crowd. The earthman took three rapid steps across the room and intercepted the boy.

"Whoa, sonny, you don't want to go in there."

"Let me go, barbarian," the boy whined, a premonition of horror in his voice. "My mother screamed!" T.K. looked at the boy's face and felt the nightmare encroaching again on his waking mind. The boy was every child he had ever seen in Vietnam, particularly that child.

"Tee-Kay?" Ku'zn stood beside the earthman and gently touched his arm. "I will watch the boy," she offered. T.K. mumbled "thanks" and turned back again, drawn by a morbid thirst for information.

"It is the same creature," Shoutte whispered as he knelt beside the body to make an examination.

"You mean one of the same kind that killed the family and those horse… uh… vorn thieves?" T.K. asked.

"No." Shoutte shook his head with great solemnity. "This is the same shadowbeast. No two creatures could be so exact in the pattern of their destruction."

The earthman forced himself to look at the shredded remains of the woman. It did indeed look like the work of the same creature, for the pattern of the claw marks across the throat and back were distinct.

"It'd be easy for it to get ahead of us the way the wagon road twisted and turned," T.K. mumbled, "but what lousy twist of fate decided we run into it three times?"

"You know this creature?" the Assassin asked. For the first time T.K. realized that it was a female voice coming from behind the black mask.

"Only by reputation," T.K. said grimly. "Haven't had the dubious pleasure of meeting it personally."

Kwa Tan, the husband of the slain woman, pushed his way past Ku'zn and took two steps into the stable before he saw the corpse. He halted, his jaw slack, and attempted to speak but no words came out.

Meanwhile Shoutte rose, eyes fixed on the victim and unawares of the husband. "If this shadowbeast haunts us, it is by design," the priest said. "Such creatures do not exist but to satisfy the foul whim of some warp wizard. We must ask ourselves what it is that we possess or are that would draw such to us…" Then he saw the husband and grieving son and stopped himself abruptly.

"Come," Shoutte whispered gently to Kwa Tan, taking the man by the arm, "let us move into the common room. Your son needs you." T.K. and the Assassin followed, pulling the doors closed behind them.

"What is going on?" a night-robe clad Lord Rayjol demanded. He wore a long sleeping cap on his head that trailed behind him like a mane.

T.K. snapped his head in the direction of the man intending a vitriolic reply but caught sight of a very frightened Zulla standing beside the man, a bright blanket wrapped around her.

"Uh-there's been a death," the earthman said as gently as possible. "It was Lady Kwa." The woman's son choked back a cry and ran to Kwa Tan.

"Father?" he pleaded.

Tannilee gasped in genuine shock. "What happened to my lady?"

"It appears she was killed by a wild beast," Shoutte said. "But that is not of concern now—she has made her transition. We must attend to the living." He looked over at the husband and son. "I have herbs in my room to calm them."

"Wait a minute, Erique," T.K. said. "The animal that did this is probably still here inside somewhere."

"Inside?" Zulla repeated fearfully.

"Yeah," T.K. continued. "Would you go back out into that?" He jerked his thumb to indicate the roaring Z'last clawing at the skylight above them.

"What's going o—Zulla!" The innkeeper halted so abruptly coming down the stairs that the sleepy eyed Orancha, following him wrapped in a blanket, almost collided with him. "What is going on here, daughter?" he recovered quickly.

"A woman has been killed by an animal, father," she replied.

"If that animal is still in the inn," the Princess commanded, "I want it caught and killed." She spoke with such absolute assurance, that it had only to be ordered to be done, that most in the room looked at her with odd expressions.

"Well, dolts," Rayjol said, "do as her highness commands." He was not an inspiring figure; with his long cap and a sleep mask pushed up on his forehead, he looked distinctly like a circus clown.

T.K. and Erique exchanged a look as if to say, "*Do you want to hit him or shall I?*" but then Shoutte shrugged.

T.K. stepped toward the chamberlain with a grim expression that forecast violence. Rayjol cringed.

"You almost make royal sense," the earthman said. "We have to set up a search pattern and sweep this place to get that shadow critter before it gets any more of us."

Rayjol recovered his composure and attempted to stare T.K. down. "Even you make sense, upstart, but the Princess must have utmost security."

"Most certainly, Lord Rayjol," Shoutte agreed. "We will break into groups and her highness can remain here in a safe area. I will go for the herbs." He smiled. "Any shadowbeast will find I have my own formidable fang." He patted Rhythemwand.

"So sure, warrior-priest?" the Assassin asked.

"Wait a minute," T.K. said, halting the priest. "We'll all need someone to watch our backs. Non-combatants stay here with King Kong." He nodded toward Conkull.

"But where do we look?" Adriana asked.

"Everywhere," Lord Shoutte said. "We have no clear idea of what this shadow creature looks like, its size or habits. It might have slipped by us into the upper levels."

"That's it, tigers," T.K. spoke to Ku'zn and Adriana. "Get yourselves a weapon, then you two go through the stable, carefully." He patted the ever-attentive Toto beside him. "You go with them, Toto."

"I will take the upper corridor," Shoutte offered. "That way I can get the herbs as well."

"Why don't you take Lady Blackpants with you," T.K. suggested. Lord Shoutte looked at the Assassin and smiled, nodding.

"Take Zul with you too," T.K. added.

"And you two," the earthman said pointing to the two brigands who were trying to blend into the furniture, "come with me to check out the ground floor."

"Wait just a moment," Olzen said with indignation. "What gives you the right to order us around like this?"

"Yes," the chubby Jonzun added. "By what right?" T.K. looked at the two of them as if he were thinking of spanking them.

"Any more stupid questions?" he ignored the half-begun objections of the two bandits. No one else in the room spoke, each setting their thoughts to the search ahead. To one side Kwa Tan sobbed quietly in his son's arms.

Everyone turned to leave, silently splitting into their search groups. Even the two bandits moved over by T.K. prepared to do their duty. He shooed the two bandits ahead of him toward the kitchen. Adriana picked up a cast iron skillet for her weapon and she and Ku'zn opened the double doors to the stable.

"I will go with you, Tee-Kay," little Zulla called out suddenly. "I know this place well and will show you the way." She crossed the room and stood beside the earthman, looking up at him.

"I forbid it, daughter," Zul said from the landing above, "It will be— dangerous."

"She'll be alright, pop," T.K. said glad to have friendly company. "I'll keep an eye on her, I promise." It seemed the wrong thing to say, for Zul started back down the stairs but was stopped by Lord Shoutte.

"She will be safe with him, innkeeper," Shoutte said. "Let us find this creature." The man shot his daughter a disapproving look and then lead his party through the arch.

"This way, Tee-Kay," the girl said with a note of triumph in her voice, "you'll protect me, won't you?" He smiled down at her.

"'Course I will, Pumpkin, but only if you protect me." She nodded a very serious yes.

"For as long as I can," she whispered earnestly. "As long as you'll let me."

The kitchen of Dragonthroat was what T.K. decided was a Flintstones-modern-industrial. Ceramic pipes brought hot and cold water from underground springs to the stone sink off to the right. Beyond that were two close-weave rush doors to the right rear of the room. To the left was counter space and cabinets, carved out of rock and topped with slabs of wood.

Two boiling pits, great stone basins with fire pits built beneath them, occupied most of the back wall along with a smaller fire pit for broiling and several racks of bowls and cups.

Along the center of the room at waist height was a counter piled high with kitchen paraphernalia, effectively blocking vision into half of the room.

"Stay behind me, Pumpkin," T.K. said quietly, "but stay close."

"All right," Zula whispered, stepping closer.

The glowgems in the room had all been night veiled, leaving the room painted with shadows that gave ominous shape to simple objects. T.K. motioned the two bandits to circle the counter at one end while he circled the other.

"I don't like this," Jonzun stage whispered to his partner. "It's dangerous."

"We should have just waited in the common room until the storm goes away," Olzen protested.

"These storms go on for days, right Zulla?" T.K. said in a tired voice.

"Yes, sometimes a ten-day."

"You guys really want to stay awake for a week-and-a-half," he asked, "never knowing when this thing will strike?" The two brigands looked in defeat at each other and then nervously moved around the counter.

All moved slowly, their bare or slippered feet making dull sounds on the cool stone floor. Jonzun nearly had a heart attack when he kicked a metal pot, but otherwise the walk down the length of the kitchen was uneventful. At last they stood by the two woven doors.

"Okay, heroes," T.K. said and smiled at the two, "after you."

+++

Upstairs Lord Shoutte and the Assassin led Zul. When they reached the priest's room Lord Shoutte went in, Rhythemwand drawn. He went to his healer's bag and retrieved thodist powder sedative and a few other herbs he thought he might need. The other two watched from the doorway.

"Have you seen wounds like that woman's before?" the Assassin asked Zul. The innkeeper was startled at first that the thin black shape beside him had spoken; he quickly shook his head. "Why no, what do you mean?"

"I have seen and caused much death in my life," the Assassin said in a cold whisper, "but never one which left marks like those; the priest mentioned a Shadow beast…"

"Death is common everywhere," Zul interrupted, "but I have never seen marks their like before." He spoke with almost ferocious finality just as Shoutte stepped into the corridor. "As to Wizard beasts," the innkeeper declared, "I'll have none of them or their pit spawned masters."

"HAVE YOU SEEN WOUNDS LIKE THAT WOMAN'S BEFORE?"

"Two rooms more," Shoutte whispered as he led them down the hall. He held Rhythemwand before him in challenge. The Assassin moved behind him to his right, never quite out of the priest's sight, and Zul walked two steps back to the left.

One of the rooms left was the small latrine that consisted of several stone chairs (minus bottoms) over an angled shaft, where run off from the hot spring ran in a constant waterfall. The room proved empty, but the Assassin made a point of carefully inspecting the slide for signs of handholds.

"It has been known to have been used for concealment," she said by way of explanation. That left only the last room on the floor, the hot spring room.

All three halted, a tense expectancy holding them in the doorway. "This is nonsense," Zul blurted out and pushed passed the two warriors. "The creature is obviously not here."

He went ahead into the room and the two others looked at each other with questions. "After you," the Assassin said to Shoutte, her almond shaped ice blue eyes smiling.

Shoutte smiled back. "I'd rather not be in front of your blades," he whispered, "if you do not mind."

"The time will come," she said and stepped into the room to find it empty save for Zul.

"The creature must be below then," Shoutte observed. "We had best go down." He started to leave, and then motioned for the Assassin to lead. She laughed and led the way at a brisk walk.

+++

In the kitchen the four searchers had toured the rooms where Zul and his daughter lived, which were reached through one of the woven rush doors. Now the quartet stood before the other door.

"This is the last room then," T.K. said. "The lady or the tiger."

"What?" Zulla asked.

"Just, if it's here, it's in there." He started for the door latch.

"Don't go in there," Zulla said, suddenly frightened. "I have a bad feeling about it."

"Easy, Pumpkin. You said it's only the food larder and the entrance to the fungus farm you talked about, right?" She nodded but with no conviction when he added, "And the boogieman may be at the other end of the inn."

"I've never liked that place," she said in a small voice, "I've had nightmares about it." Her eyes were pleading and the earthman paused.

T.K. thought back to some of the drawings he had seen in the young girl's simple furnished room. Among the stylized drawings of little animals were several pictures of fearsome imaginary beasts. He wondered if what they faced could indeed be standing on the other side of the flimsy door and if it looked anything like the razor-toothed monstrosities of her imaginings. He shuddered.

"It'll be alright, babe," he insisted, more to convince himself than her. "Abbott and Costello here will back me up. Right guys?" The two bandits, not pleased with the prospect, nonetheless nodded yes.

"So then," T.K. said, "this'll only take a minute." He pushed in the door with a rush and quickly unveiled the glowgems to the right of the door. A frantic and dreaded search proved the storeroom empty.

"We must have scared it away," Jonzun said with deliberate joy, and just a touch of bravado.

"Maybe not," T.K. cautioned quietly. "We haven't tried there." He pointed to the wood slab door at the back of the room Zulla had said lead to an abandoned copper mine her father had converted into a mushroom and fungus farm.

"It can't be," Olzen said with relief, "see, the door is barred on this side." It was true. The bolt to the door was closed and locked. At that moment Lord Shoutte entered the storeroom from the kitchen followed by the Assassin and Zul.

"The upstairs is all clear, friends."

"Then the damn thing's gotta be in the stable." T.K. stated. The group turned and headed straight into the common room at a run. All that is, save for the two bandits who lingered to collect a few snacks for later.

In the common room Ku'zn and Adriana were waiting for the hunting party. "Be at ease," the Z'n said, "we found a burrow hole near the outer wall. It must have gotten out the same way it got in."

"We piled a ten-weight of boards and feed bags atop the hole," Adriana added. "It will not be able to enter that way again."

Everyone sheathed their weapons and visibly relaxed.

"Whew!" T.K. voiced the thoughts of everyone in the room. "Let's get some brews, party down and pass out."

"Well," Tannilee said casting a dissenting vote, "aren't you going to go after it?"

Even Lord Rayjol ignored the remark and moved to confer with Shoutte about Kwa Tan and his son. When she realized no one was listening to her, the princess left, trying not to look flustered. A perplexed Conkull followed her.

Zul produced a jug of wine and poured a round of nightcaps for everyone while Lord Shoutte attended to the husband and the boy who were in shock. He accompanied both to their room where he sent the man and boy to bed heavily drugged and under the chamberlain's care.

After he had attended to the two Shoutte returned to accept a tankard from the earthman then whispered to T.K., "I swear this shadowbeast is a plague to haunt me, as if I needed to be reminded of my blood oath."

Shoutte then joined the four contractors, T.K. and Zulla for a final tankard of wine. Zul went off to secure the body of the slaughtered woman in the cool confines of the fungus farm. Everyone else had returned to bed with uneasy steps.

Above the storm raged unabated, clawing at the skylight and howling contemptuously as if angry there was a place it could not reach.

"I wish we had never come to this awful place," Zulla said with quiet frustration. She had a small cup of watered wine and pushed it around the table in a distracted way. "I miss trees and flowers; you don't ever see them around here." The young girl consoled herself by petting a happily hissing Toto who had placed his iridescent head in her lap.

"Where are you from, Zulla?" Lord Shoutte inquired. "I thought you were of Cosen."

"No," she made a face, "We're from Mephan. Father was a cutter in the butchers guild, but after mother died he purchased this station through a guild brother in Tolan." The teenager became suddenly embarrassed at being the center of attention and her cheeks flushed with color.

"All Mephans are butchers," Ku'zn mumbled under her breath. She was huddled in T.K.'s arms with her head against his shoulder, well into her cups. The earthman winced at the unbridled hatred in her tones.

I'm pure Mephan if that Meegana dame is to be believed, T.K. thought. *So I guess I'd better not discuss family trees with Peachfuzz for a while.*

He felt a little dishonest with his new friends not to have mentioned the strange woman to them and now to keep her information a secret, but a long career of honesty had netted him mostly black eyes. He decided in the interest of peace to be quiet about both facts for at least a little while longer.

"I think we have all had enough excitement this one night to last for quite some time," Lord Shoutte murmured. "I suggest we get as much rest as we can." There was a general consent all around and everyone rose. Adriana and Lunit left first, followed by Yomi.

"Good night, Pumpkin," T.K. gave Zulla an affectionate peck on the top of her head. "Things'll look better tomorrow." When she didn't look too sure he added, "I want to do that portrait of you in the morning so you have to get your beauty sleep." That comment set her to giggling and she waved as he and Ku'zn went up the stairs arm in arm with Toto their caboose.

"Funny, I don't feel the least bit sleepy," the earthman said to the Z'n.

"Neither do I," she said suggestively. "Fear does that to me to."

"Not fear," those below heard him say as they disappeared into the upper corridor, "Professional caution…"

"Good night, sir priest," Zulla said clearing the table and heading for the kitchen.

"And to you, Blossom," Shoutte smiled, "Remember that change is constant—that is the way of the Kova. Things will be better."

"Thank you, sir," she said more hopefully. "Good night."

Lord Shoutte stood in the center of the room and watched the teen 'til she was in the kitchen, then said in a deadly sharp whisper, "Into the light, skulker."

A section of shadow near the stable door resolved itself into the Assassin.

"I am tired, madam," the priest said, "but tomorrow we will find some privacy and discuss why you violated Pax in my room tonight. I do not want to see you until then. If I do, I will kill you." With that the priest calmly ascended the stairs.

Beneath her mask and hood, the Assassin smiled coldly and followed him up the stairs, looking forward to the morrow with carnivorous joy.

Chapter Ten

"Everything looks good in a heap by the bed."
Wolff's first law of fashion

The rest of the night at Dragonthroat was uneventful and all the guests slept more or less peacefully. Except T.K. Mitchell.

The former Marine's sleep, when at last Ku'zn and Adriana let him sleep, was once again troubled. Jagged edges and violent colors slashed through his dreams though the nightmare was distant now, as if in the background of a new horror. He was roused suddenly just before dawn by an explosion of red in his past and awoke covered in a cold sweat.

Damn, he thought as he extracted himself from between the two women. *Even booze doesn't work after a night like last night.* He rose quietly, slipped on a pair of buckskin breeches and strapped on his ankle brace that was sitting on a low table by the door. He slipped on his moccasins then paused at the door.

Toto, sleeping at the foot of the bed, hissed in his sleep and rolled over, his eyes suddenly open and staring at T.K. The earthman smiled wearily back at the animal and whispered.

"It's okay, Toto—just a guilty conscience and a need to take a whiz. Go back to sleep." The creature seemed to understand and let his head settle back to the ground and was soon asleep again.

From the doorway T.K. looked back at his two companions who were deep in dreamless sleep; the blue-furred Ku'zn coiled in a fetal position like a giant sexy teddy bear, and the long-limbed Adriana stretched out on her back, her right ebony leg hanging off the stone platform.

Man, what a trip! he thought with a grin. *I could never have dreamed this up on the best of Haight-Ashbury's finest.*

He shook his head unable to really believe the events of the past three days. Moreover, he was annoyed with himself for feeling so confortable on Altiva. *It's too freakin' weird,* he told himself. *I don't want to get comfortable here; it has too much death.* Yet, he felt as if he were renewing old acquaintances, with Shoutte and the women, particularly Ku'zn. It annoyed him to no end. *I don't want any friends, particularly old ones.*

I need a drink, he decided as he closed the door to the room behind him. *But first I gotta get rid of some beer.* The corridor was chilly and quiet. He seemed to be the only one awake and abroad. He walked briskly toward the privy, but just as he reached the entrance something in the spring room caught his attention.

An intermittent glow was coming from the room. T.K. watched for a moment and then, despite his need to relieve himself, moved toward the glow. "I'll probably hate myself in the morning for doing this," he mumbled as he entered the spring room.

The room appeared to be empty, but T.K. was cautious while moving to the edge of the pool and peering into the calm water. He saw nothing unusual except, that even with the room's glowgems night-veiled, the room was daylight bright.

Weird, he concluded, then turned to answer his bladder's command and almost toppled over backwards in fright. There, standing in the doorway to the room, was the warp wizard woman, Meegana Rakkdon.

"Jeez, lady," T.K. moaned. "Will you stop doing that!" The woman barely came to T.K.'s shoulder, yet under the force of her piercing eyes, he felt dwarfed by her. She stood with her arms at her sides, her hands, save for her delicate fingertips, hidden by the sleeves of her blood-colored robe.

"I have come to warn you of great danger," the woman said impassively.

"Better get another watch," T.K. sneered. "You're an hour late."

"The danger is still near," she said ominously. "The wizard-emperor's wrath can take many forms." She stared hard at him and the resulting chill that the earthman felt was immediately relayed to his urinary tract.

"Yeah, okay, fine." He hopped from foot to foot. "Look, Meg, I gotta go, you know? Gotta drain the lizard. Can we talk about this later?"

"There is no time," she began.

"You're telling me?"

"I believe," she interrupted, the impatience clear in her voice, "that Roosuf summoned this Z'last by means arcane, either to kill you outright or drive you directly to the inn of Dragonthroat."

"That's nice." T.K. shuffled more erratically. "Can we please talk later—these are the only buckskins I own?"

"By the Twins, have you no spine, Teel Kantos?"

"None—but I do have a mighty fine bladder—"

"To think that the blood of emperors runs in your veins!" she said in disgust.

"That's not all that'll be running if you don't let me go." His voice was desperate.

"Have you no sense of duty to your ancestors? Rossuf must be stopped."

"Listen, I don't want the job. I am no longer a leader of men, or tveks or Z'n for that matter. I don't care about Roosuf and I don't want to care about your bloody painful world. I don't even give a damn about the one I come from, lady. They're both ruled by stupidity and red tape but at least the mess back home was familiar. I screwed up there and I screw up here and I screw up anywhere I get drunk—and I get drunk everywhere I can."

He started to move toward her, concluding, "Right now I want to piss and go home in that order so get out of my way." He reached out to brush her aside but his hand passed through her image, causing it to waver like smoke.

"Roosuf's power is strong, Teel Kantos—not to be ignored." Her voice faded to sound as if it were far away. "Much as you try you cannot deny your blood. The monster Rosuff will hunt you down and slay you because he must, to protect his position. As well he must keep you from becoming a rallying point for those that oppose him. There is no escape from that; he would have tracked you down on that other world of yours had I not brought you back for you to have a chance to oppose him. For the love I bore your mother, the princess, I must prevent him from his purpose. Much as I might agree that you are not suited for this is the only course of action."

Her image and voice began to dissipate even more as she continued. "I can not come to you directly so will not reach you for some days. Be on guard—-Roosuf's schemes for evil are like a muddy river, dark treacherous and inexorable. Beware things that are not as they seem—-" Then the image of the wizardess was gone and so was the former marine, dashing at flank speed for the water closet.

+++

T.K. made his way to the common room unable to even consider sleep after his encounter with Meegana. He brought his notebook down with him and spent some time with Toto finding where Zul kept his private stock of beer.

"You'd be a damn alky, if I wasn't here to save you, Toto, me'lad," he said to the tvek as he sat down at a table in the common room. He poured a bowl for the tvek who began to lap it up immediately. "Drinkin' by your self is the first sign you have a problem, Toto, old fellow." He laughed. "Followed by talking to yourself."

He opened his journal and began the process of recording the night's events, hoping along the way to sort out some of them. After an hour of writing, however, he was nowhere near being able to understand it all so he began to draw while he thought. *Three days on this world and so much death, but so much life too. It just doesn't seem the sort of place that lets you take a passive stand on living. You can't just stand by and let the world flow around you, you have to participate. And I'd gotten real good at just coasting along, not doin' Jack for what, eight years? What is this—tornado shock therapy? And what about this Meegana dame? Half the time I expect her to sing Bippidy Boppity Boo,"* the other half to turn me into a frog. *Man, it's so unreal. Me, an emperor? That is the biggest joke of it all. Emperor? Sure!*

"You are up early, Tee Kay." Zulla's voice from behind him startled the Earthman into dropping his drawing pen and brought Toto out of a drowse with a growling hiss. The young girl was standing in the doorway to the kitchen tying on her apron.

"Oh, morning, Pumpkin. Shut up, Toto!" He smiled. "I couldn't sleep."

She nodded. "Yes, I had trouble sleeping too, I had nightmares again."

"It's understandable after last night," he said quietly.

"Did you?" she asked.

"No more than usual." She stepped closer and looked down at him intensely.

"You have too kind a face to dream of demons and death, Tee Kay." There was so much sincerity in her comment that T.K. blushed.

"What about you, Pumpkin? You should only be dreaming of high school football heroes or you'll end up wrinkled like a prune."

"What is football?" she asked with great interest.

"Football," he said after some thought, "is either a sport or an excuse to gamble, depending on who you ask. In either case you stand a good chance to get kneecapped."

She considered for a moment then asked, "Will I really get wrinkles from bad dreams?"

He laughed. "Like a prune."

"Prune?" she questioned. She stepped closer to peer down at his journal where he had finished a drawing of Lord Shoutte and his vorn.

"I did not know you made pictures so well," she said a little awed. "It is like 'craft. It looks so like the priest."

"Aw, just another useless talent," he declared, "I've got hundreds of them." Then he laughed gently. "They started me out drawing still lives of fruit at the veteran's hospital as therapy; it beat basket weaving, and the instructor was this cute hippie girl. Anyway, I had a knack for it so I took some classes here and there." He finished the last detail on the drawing and held it up to the light of the glowgems.

"Wonderful," she whispered.

"Not too shabby at that," he agreed. He set the book down and nodded when the teenager indicated she wanted to look through it.

"I wish I could picture so well," she said wistfully.

"You'll do a lot better than me if you just keep at it. You've got a head start and a good eye." She didn't look liked she believed him.

"Tell you what though," he suggested, "if you let me do that drawing of you I'll play art teacher while I'm here."

Her answer was to launch herself at him like a friendly flying octopus and squeal "You will, you will?" in his ear. When he laughed yes, she began to giggle, grabbing on twice as tight and stealing away his breath.

But when the laughter was played out and both were breathless she did not release her hold on him—she only relaxed it.

All of a sudden the earthman became aware of the heat radiating from the young girl's body and an answering heat from his own body. Her breasts pressed flat against his chest and, separated from him by only two layers of fabric seemed to ignite a secondary fire, warming his skin and the blood beneath.

She seemed to sense the moment of awaking on some intuitive level, and drew in a sharp breath, looking up at him to fix him in her eyes. She had eyes so green and clear that he could see all the way to the bottom of her soul, to the unopened space of her innocence. It called to him both in challenge and in sincerity. It said "Tee Kay?" softly in her voice.

"Uh, oh, what, Pumpkin?" he asked, returning his focus to the surface of her eyes.

"You looked so—so strange," she said with concern. "Is everything alright?"

"Yes, Zulla," he said easing her arms from around him. "Everything is fine, unspoiled the way it should be." He took a deep breath and changed to a playful tone. He kissed her on the forehead.

"Now, my little unstill life—get comfortable in that chair over there so I can immortalize you." With that he set about recording both the way that Zulla looked and how she affected him.

He sketched her in colored chalk using two pages from his journal book, humming Led Zeppelin tunes while he drew. He talked to her softly, telling her simple jokes and rambling a little about his travels. When he was finished with the portrait she was delighted beyond words at his skill and he even had to admit he had captured a good likeness of the gamin.

Later he submitted to posing for her and was pleased with her version of his craggy smile. He began his art lessons for her with studies of light and shade on Toto's face. And this is how Zul found the three of them an hour later, with the two humans bent over a drawing of a besotted tvek.

"Zulla," her father said in a deep stern voice. "Go in the kitchen and get your work done. We do have other guests."

"Yes, father," she said quietly, then turned to kiss T.K. on the cheek. "Thank you for the art lessons, Tee-Kay," she said with a blush, and then hurried out of the room.

Zul remained in the doorway, his piercing gaze locked on T.K. The earthman returned the steady gaze with indignation, wearing his virtue like armor. At last the innkeeper 'harrumphed' and turned to attend the kitchen.

"Man," T.K. told Toto when they were alone, "I finally come down firmly on the path of righteousness, and I get the hairy eyeball for it from the old man. I've got to stop getting myself into these situations." He looked down at the tvek for reassurance but the animal merely burped from his beer.

"You said it, boy," T.K. turned back to a study of Ku'zn he had started the night before. Soon he was lost in another drawing.

"Absorbed?" Lord Shoutte's whisper startled T.K. out of his drawing almost an hour later. "Oh, good likeness." Shoutte wore a crystal tiara-like headband and was dressed in a white silk robe embroidered with gold cloth bearing the triple diamond symbol of his religion.

"'Morning, Erique. You slept late."

Shoutte smiled, "Not really, I just got out of bed late."

"Limits, reverend father, limits!" T.K. laughed. "Why all dolled up?"

"I have attended the boy and his father already this morning," Shoutte said with solemnity. "Now I must attend the mother below, anoint the body with spices and perform a transition ceremony for her."

The thought of the previous night's violence cast a shadow over the two men. Shoutte, however, soon brightened. "By the Rhythem, Tee-Kay," Shoutte advised, "it is the way of life, however harsh. It is why we savor each breath so—"

"Please, no homilies before breakfast, Erique," T.K. said. Shoutte's answering smile held only the merest hint of condescension.

"As you wish," Shoutte said and then went into the kitchen, passing a sleepy eyed Orancha on her way out.

"Morning," T.K. called out to her. She winced at the noise and slowly made her way over to his table. "Grab a seat," he whispered. She collapsed onto the bench opposite him.

"Curse Juva ale," she said softly. "It sneaks up on you around the fourth bottle." T.K. nodded understandingly and offered a mug of his ale.

"A little hair of the dog should fix you up."

She picked up the mug and peered into it quizzically.

"Dag?" she whispered looking for alien animal hair in the drink.

"Never mind. Just hold up 'til I get some more for myself, then drink away and I'll race you to oblivion."

Oblivion for the earthman never arrived, for a breakfast of roast meat, hot cereal, and dried fruit soon brought a full house into the common room. The groups stayed to themselves, the princess and her reduced entourage took up two corner tables, with Kwa Tan and his son obviously under heavy sedation. The bandits were jolly after a night's sleep and the still silent Assassin seemed to just appear in her now usual seat against the wall.

"Pass those fruit chips, Smurfette," T.K. asked of Ku'zn. The blue-furred woman gave him the dish without shifting her gaze from Tannilee's table. T.K. followed her gaze to young Kwa Chen.

"Yeah, pretty bad about the boy," he said. "He came in here a while ago and just stared into the stables with that look on his face. We used to call it the "Life Sucks" look in my unit. We saw it on a lot of faces in 'Nam."

"I wore that face myself when Mephistal raiders attacked my village and slew my blood mother," Ku'zn said quietly. "My brother Ka'wn carried me for days without rest until we were safe—I would have died from mother's loss alone if he had not comforted me. It is not a good time to be alone." She kept her eyes turned toward the boy but her focus was on a long ago beach.

"Go ahead, Peachfuzz," T.K. said gently pushing her toward the boy. "It'll make a difference; you did for me at the hill farm." The Z'n woman smiled a 'thanks for understanding' smile and rose to head across the room.

"One thing," she whispered before she left, "Peachfuzz I kind of like but don't call me a Smoofit. I don't think I like that."

"No problem." He laughed as she walked away. *Life indeed sucks*, he said to himself looking at her comforting the boy, *but there are those that give it moments of unsuck.*

Toto, seated patiently on the floor beside the earthman, looked up and hissed in apparent agreement that brought another laugh from T.K.

At the royal table Lord Rayjol leaned over to listen to a whispered command from the princess, shook his head in violent disagreement, and then withered under a regal stare. Then the chamberlain rose and headed straight for the earthman.

"Sirrah," Rayjol said in a diffident voice, "Her Royal Highness requires your attendance." The man stood expectantly to T.K.'s right ready for flight or faint at the earthman's slightest movement.

"Bug off, weasel beak." T.K. mumbled through a mouthful of food. The chamberlain looked stricken and his pale skin went pure white.

"Perhaps, Sirrah, you did not understand," Rayjol said, recovering somewhat from his shock. "You have been summoned by royal order." He inclined his head in a slight bow.

T.K. smiled, returned the bow and said in a pleased voice. "Perhaps you don't understand—I don't give a flying tvek, and you are a royal pain!" Rayjol's eyes all but crossed with rage and apoplectic indecision at the earthman's blasphemous remark.

"Sirrah," he hissed in a wounded tone only to bring an answering hiss from Toto.

"No 'sirrah', Bozo," T.K. said, "Mister. And if Tannilee wants to talk to me she has two functioning legs of her own. Tell her to use them."

The Chamberlain turned with all diplomatic speed and stomped across to the princess' table.

"You are not a very tactful man, are you, friend Tee-Kay?" The sultry Adriana leaned across the table to refill her ale cup. The earthman laughed coldly, all the while watching the heated discussion his refusal had engendered at the princess' table.

"I'm tactful only when it's deserved, sweetcakes," he answered. "Oh, now and again I screw up and go too far." He leaned down and gave a morsel of meat to Toto who hissed his thanks.

"I think this time you have gone too far, Tee-Kay," she continued, "for the princess has the right of death by decree the moment we leave Dragonthroat. Her father is an absolute ruler."

"Experts have tried to kill me, honey, and from what I've seen of the hired help around here, I'm in more danger of dying from either boredom or over exertion—depending on your mood later." Nonetheless he watched the whispered furor occurring at the royal table and wished he had been a bit more opaque with the Chamberlain.

"You do not fear death?" The delicate Yomi asked. "I would have thought you a wiser man than that."

"'Course I'm afraid of a lot of things," T.K. watched as the princess rose from her chair. "Of dying alone, needles, growing decrepit old, spiders. But 'Nam burnt a lot of the normal fears, like just plain old dying, right out of me. Death ain't nothing special, it happens every day in a hundred ways; just part of life. It's all in how and when you go, and I hope to pick both, and how you live that matters."

The princess tried to make her approach look casual and calm. T.K. watched her while he continued to ramble. "I've never been one for red tape either, or top brass type ordering people around for no good reason and treating you like dirt but not hesitating to use you if they need you."

"That kind of attitude must make you very unpopular if you stay in one place too long," Adriana observed.

"Yeah, well sometimes I feel like I've been wandering my whole life. I even tried settling down once before the war. It didn't work then, can't work now. Something to do with trust I think—can't trust or be trusted."

There was a moment of pained silence at the table and then Zulla, who had been standing nearby at the fire pit, said with a quiet conviction, "You can trust me, Tee Kay, I trust you completely."

Before T.K. had a chance to absorb or answer the young girl's comment Princess Tannilee of Cosen was upon him in full regal fury. "How dare you ignore a royal summons, Sirrah!" Behind the princess loomed the muscular Conkull.

"How dare you ignore even the illusion of civility," T.K. said. "I come from a country without royalty so we have this romantic concept that royalty means graceful!"

Everyone at the table froze. The room hushed.

Olzen immediately bet his croney that last night's dancing lesson would be repeated.

Conkull growled and was cut off short by a wave of Tannilee's hand.

"We would have you walk with us," Princess Tannilee said in an amazingly restrained voice. She held the royal right hand out to T.K. and he was so taken aback at the turnabout in her attitude that he took the hand and rose to walk beside her.

"Let us walk to the stables," she suggested.

The giant barbarian followed behind the two of them like an obedient but dangerous puppy until the princess signaled him to remain at the entrance to the stable with a wave of her hand.

T.K. decided on parity. "You stay here too, Toto," he said to the tvek, which had also followed. "I'll whistle if I need you."

T.K. allowed Tannilee to pass through the doorway ahead of him and for a moment he and Conkull made eye contact. The barbarian's expression was more a promise than a threat and T.K.'s look returned it in kind. "Watch him, Toto," the earthman said, "but be careful if you have to bite him, I see rabies on the horizon from him."

"Now, sirrah," Tannilee snapped in a sharp voice as the stable door closed behind them.

She turned to face T.K. and as she did, she slapped the unprepared man across the face. "You will not refuse a direct order from our person again!"

T.K. was so stunned by her imperious rage that he just stared at her.

"That, sirrah will be the end to all that," she decided.

The Princess turned away from the earthman certain beyond doubt that he was completely cowed by her sudden shift of tactics. "As to why I called you, sirrah, we admired your martial arts skill and prowess last evening. After some thought, we have decided that your services would be advisable as additional escort on the remainder of our journey to the capital."

She paused dramatically, facing away from T.K. with arms akimbo, head inclined thoughtfully. T.K. contained himself for only a moment before bursting out laughing. He laughed so hard that he began to cry.

The princess went livid white.

"Easy, Princess," T.K. managed between wracking laughs, "no major offense meant. It's, uh… just that the last thing I expected was for you to offer me is a job!" Her expression of rage gradually melted into understanding of the irony, allowing her a truly amused smile.

"Then it is settled. You will take service with us." It was a statement.

"Don't get mad," he said soberly, "but I'm already working for Orancha's Choir, at least as far as Tolan." Before she could pout or become angry again he added, "But much as my stomach tells me otherwise, there's safety in numbers. We are headed the same place you are. No reason the two groups can't travel together and I promise to keep an extra eye out on you. Does that satisfy?"

She considered for a moment then nodded assent. "You will henceforth address our person with proper respect."

T.K. bowed elaborately. "You shall receive all the respect you deserve." He spoke with a wide Cheshire Cat smile.

Tannilee decided her royal honor had been satisfied and let her mantel of authority fall away for a moment. "The journey will be good with you along," she said with total lack of affectation. "Both the Princess of Cosen and Tannilee will feel much more safe."

T.K. touched by her statements, nodded a warm 'thank you,' then he rubbed his cheek. "Just one thing though," he added, "everyone gets only one free shot at me, Princess, and you've had yours, so let's keep this all on the up and up from here on out, okay?"

The line of her smile hardened for a moment and she extended her hand palm down. T.K. recognized what she wanted and bent to do his best Errol Flynn impersonation to touch his lips to the knuckles. It satisfied her and she left the hand there for him to take. "Let us return to the others," she said with good humor. "We have kept them waiting in suspense long enough."

"Yeah, they expect one of us to come back in with the other's head on a platter." She joined him in a laugh.

Think you have a new pet dog all you want, Tanni' baby, but don't forget I've got teeth.

The common room's occupants continued subdued conversations, feigning disinterest (except for Jonzun, who cursed under his breath and handed a few coins to Olzen) when T.K. and Tannilee reentered the room, arm in arm and smiling.

"Our conversation has been of great interest, Tee-Kay," the princess said with enough volume for all to hear as he moved to sit at his table. "We shall speak further on the road to Tolan."

"Anytime, Tanni-cakes. Your Highness" he added quickly. "The door is always open."

She smiled regally and turned back to her table. In the process she stepped on the long hem of her gown and stumbled, taking a very un-regal nosedive into a bowl of porridge on the center server.

T.K. and Conkull both made it to her side at the same time, but the earthman deferred to the barbarian, who spent several seconds trying to figure out how to help the princess up without touching her. Failing to find a way he simply grabbed her about the waist and lifted her completely off the ground to clear her feet of the entangled gown.

Jonzun burst out laughing when he saw the usually immaculate princess with the porridge facial. Most in the room had more restraint.

"Release me, you dolt!" Tannilee screamed in frustration. She pushed passed the giant and stumbled up stairs muttering to herself. Rayjol and the rest of her party raced out after her, all save Conkull who lingered at the bottom of the stairs.

"You will not laugh at the Princess of Cosen," he commanded the room. This seemed to set Jonzun off again and he convulsed with laughter.

"Silence, tvek dung, or feel the wrath of Conkull of Krinaria." The poor bandit was helpless to stop his fit, so it was up to Olzen to step between the two.

"My companion meant no offense," he said quickly, elbowing Jonzun to silence. "He has an affliction."

"It's truth, sir," the gasping Jonzun said. "I simply have an antic nature."

"Just so," Olzen piped in, "he is subject to periodic fits, this one just had unfortunate timing."

"Well," Conkull said after ponderous consideration, "quiet him."

T.K., who had watched the exchange with fiendish delight, could

...TAKING AN UN-REGAL NOSEDIVE INTO A BOWL OF PORRIDGE...

no longer restrain himself. "They're making fun of you, big guy," the earthman noted with a concerned voice, "I don't think they respect you."

The two bandits shot T.K. a terrified look and a suddenly very sober Jonzun insisted, "No, no. We have the greatest respect and admirations for Krinarians, especially you, sirrah."

"Absolutely," Jonzun added.

"That's a joke, Connie baby," T.K. rested a friendly hand on the giant's huge bicep. "Why, didn't you see that gesture the fat one made when the princess left?"

"Sir!" Jonzun squealed, "Your comments are not appreciated."

"What gesture?" Conkull demanded.

"That's a problem I've always had," T.K. said, "I've never been truly appreciated.

"What gesture?" Conkull bellowed.

"There was no gesture!" Olzen insisted.

"Oh yes there was," Ku'zn suddenly chimed in, "but it would be rude of a lady like myself to repeat it." She looked at T.K. who worked very hard not to laugh.

Conkull exploded into fury, reaching for the two bandits who screamed and raced into the kitchen. T.K. 'accidentally'got in Conkull's way, slowing his pursuit so the two bandits had a couple of seconds head start before the barbarian raced into the room after them.

A moment later there was a loud crash from the kitchen followed by a desperate cry of "Pax!" and a bellow of rage.

Shoutte, T.K. and the five women exploded into laughter.

"You have a demon fansav in your heart, my friend," Shoutte laughed. "You must have been a horrible child."

T.K. looked hurt. "I was a little darling, though terribly misunderstood," he said. "It's just that it was beginning to look like a very dull day."

Most of the morning was spent singing bawdy ballads and playing games of chance, a passion for Shoutte. Yomi proved to have a killer instinct at strip poker, the soon-to-be rage of Altiva, introduced by T.K.

"Much as I would like to continue," Lord Shoutte took his leather pants back from the pile of the little woman's winnings, "I must attend to my vorn."

"I'll give you a hand. I have to see to the lady's animals as well," T.K. lay down a bad hand and picked up his own shirt. "This little lotus blossom snake here," he smiled at a beaming Yomi, "is going to have my fillings if we keep this up much longer."

"Be at ease, Tee-Kay," Shoutte smiled. "I would not think of depriving her of that pleasure. I will attend Madame Orancha's beasts as well." T.K. picked up his cards with a look of resignation and harrumphed at Shoutte.

"Thanks, pal. Hope you step knee deep in road apples."

Once inside the stable the priest left the door ajar so he could listen to Lunit who was singing while she enjoyed watching Yomi win.

"A warrior's heart may bleed—,
Like any other heart—,
Not guaranteed invulnerable
When love is at the start—,
No cuirass, shield or buckler
Protects his vital core,
Yet the center of a warrior
Must be of something more."

The priest mucked out the stalls and set out feed for the mounts with a smile while he listened to the red-haired songstress with a smile. He enjoyed the physical activity of the stable work, reciting Kova prayer chants happily to himself while he worked. He stayed stripped to the waist, but kept his crystal blade near at hand as was his habit while she continued.

"Honor, truth and valor
All play a major part
Yet there is still a something more
Within the warrior's heart.
The will to fight, the hope to win,
A conscience and a code,
These things habitual
To all who've
sworn to allw'se Akem.
But most of all within this being
A gentle peaceful core,
For only mad or evil men
Would ever want a war."

When she finished the song the group in the common room applauded her, and Lord Shoutte nodded. "Truth in song," he said aloud. "But sadly, too few will listen to substance of the words."

Abruptly he was aware that the stable door was closed and that he was no longer alone. "I am listening, Assassin," Shoutte whispered taking up the sword and standing apart from the stalls. "Explain."

The dark robed figure materialized from the shadows beside the door and pushed her hood back to reveal angular features and long blonde hair. "I am the wife of Lee Zan Doo." She spoke as if the statement carried great weight.

"The name means nothing to me," Shoutte whispered flatly. "Who is he and why do you draw on me?"

"Bastard son of a tvek," she hissed. "You slew him three years ago in Lutece."

Shoutte split his focus between the Assassin and his memory searching for the truth of her statement.

"Yes, remember!" she said as he considered, her tone vehement. "Lutece. A tavern called the Harp of Carpas near the waterfront. You cut him down unfairly."

"That has no truth," Shoutte insisted. "I do remember the incident. He was a contracted assassin, sent to kill the owner who was a devout Kovar, and thus one of my flock. It was my duty to protect the tavern owner, which I did."

"That was a personal affair between the owner and my husband. A matter of honor, not contract."

"It was a contrived argument," Shoutte insisted. "Your husband was in the employ of a land agent who had been refused the sale of the tavern. He challenged and we both fought fairly, face to face. Your husband died a death with honor as a warrior. Do not regret his transition—it was to the Rhythem."

The Assassin's attractive features were locked in a rigid mask of denial. "He could not have been defeated fairly by the likes of you." She drew her two crystal short swords. "I will have your heart for his life."

"This does not have to be," Shoutte insisted one last time. "It will not serve the Rhythem for there to be another death here today."

The woman laughed icily. "The Goddess of Revenge, Shirra guided you here to me," she said, "I had given up hope of finding the Kovar priest who whispered and bore the crystalsword a full ten-month ago."

Her eyes had taken on a religious shine. "I was forced here to Dragonthroat by the Z'last, and now I know it was not by chance. This was meant even at the cost of my own life for violating Pax." The Assassin began to advance slowly, and Lord Shoutte realized that the time for talk was past.

He let out a long deep sigh and focused himself through Rhythemwand. Soon he and the blade were one and the Assassin existed only as an abstract concept. He would fight with the NoMind—, the basis for his sword art.

By not being he could become... winner, loser, life or death; it mattered not, for the Rhythem would be fulfilled. He heard the voice of his swordmaster, Master Braphan telling him when he was a student, *"There is no lose when one is the sword, only contending."*

"Erique!" The door to the common room popped open and Yomi stuck her head in. "The Kwa boy needs more thodist powder," she looked puzzled. "Why have you drawn your sword?" she asked. "Is the beast back?"

Shoutte now stood apparently alone in the center of the stable, the Assassin having disappeared into the darkness as the door opened. "No, Yomi," Shoutte whispered with no hint of tension in his voice. "I was just practicing; enjoying the blade. I will be along directly."

Yomi nodded and pulled the door to as she left. The Assassin reappeared.

"This must be settled later," Shoutte declared. "If it is to be settled with finality. There are too many about now who might be injured."

The Assassin agreed. "They might interfere. Enjoy your last day on this plane and think of Lee Zan Doo each and every minute of it." Her swords were sheathed and she was through the inner door before Shoutte could reply.

"By the Rhythem," the priest exclaimed as he re-sheathed his own sword. "What wizard curse has marked this journey?"

With a crash the outer door of the stable suddenly flew open. The priest whirled to see the storm swirling in turbulent eddies about seven hunched figures, who looked as if they had been carved from a nightmare.

For the briefest moment it appeared to Shoutte as if the seven figures stood in an envelope of calm air, as if some friendly god had blown a shimmering bubble around the men to protect them from the fury of the storm. Then the men moved forward and the bubble effect was gone, leaving only the vindictive winds to flick the tattered remnants of their clothes around them.

As they moved into the mouth of the cave two of them turned to close the doors behind them, fighting the cutting winds and dust with all their strength to shut and bar it. One of the larger of the men stepped up eye to eye with Shoutte and smiled.

"How about some wine for some walking dead men," Axe said with a dark laugh. "Something to wash the dust out."

Chapter Eleven

"Life sucks, then you die and get reborn to do it all over again."
Buddha in the bar.

Dragonthroat went into an uproar of disbelief when the seven men entered the common room.

"You were outside in a Z'last and lived?" Zulla asked incredulously as the men found seats around a table.

"That's impossible," Madame Orancha insisted, "the flesh would have been stripped from your bones in a moment."

"So it would have been for lesser men, good woman," Axe said hoarsely, combing sand out of his beard with a calloused hand. "If not for this." He held up the winged serpent pendant Rosuff had sent him. "I a—acquired it from a warp wizard—had no reason to test its power until now."

"We'd have had no reason to test it at all if those two tvek spawn had been a bit slower," Skins growled.

"Enough," Mace shook a cloud of dust from his ragged travel cloak. "We will put all that to right soon enough now."

"Aye—soon," Axe added, "and when I get my hands on them I'll rip their hearts out." He smiled at Knife and Lance who nodded a cheerful agreement.

Zulla rushed tankards of ale to the seven men who downed the first round before she had gone for seconds. Zul was quick on her heels with a platter of cold meat.

"Gentlemen," the innkeeper said, "this is all the meat ready at the moment, but I shall fire some more for you on the spit." He stood back for a moment and surveyed the men with admiration.

"Wizard charm or not," Zul said, "to walk through a Z'last is a great feat. While you are in Dragonthroat your monies are no good."

"Been that way once too often," Axe laughed, "though usually they mean it a different way what say it!" The seven men and the crowd around enjoyed a laugh together.

"Where are these remarkable—oh, I see!" Tannilee spoke to Lord Shoutte as she descended the stairs. Conkull and Rayjol entered directly behind them.

"You are the ones who braved the z'last?" the princess asked when she stood before their table. Axe looked up and laughed.

"Aye, lass, we're the ones." He eyed her with a look which affixed a monetary value to her body.

"This is the Princess of Cosen!" Rayjol said. "You will show proper respect."

"Be quiet, Chamberlain," Tannilee commanded. "These men are heroes—and no doubt tired—which excuses much."

"That we are, Axey," Skins agreed. "Heroes."

"And no doubt tired." Axe laughed.

"I have brought lotion, sirs," Lord Shoutte offered, "to treat your wounds, lest they fester."

"The only wounds we have are in our purses, priest," Mace snickered. "And we saw some livestock out in that stable that can heal those. We lost our vorn when the beast attacked."

"Beast?" Zulla set down a second round of tankards.

"Aye, lass." Skins laughed, spilling ale as he did. "A great frightening thing with hide like a sword and a howl to set the soul a trembling." He took great delight in the look of horror on the teenager's face.

"I still say it was a shadowbeast," Chain, another of Axe's band, said.

"A shadowbeast?" Zulla exclaimed. "Could it have been the same one you told me of, Tee-Kay?"

"Real possible, Pumpkin," the earthman said, catching Shoutte's eye. "We seemed to have passed through the same area as these heroic gentlemen."

The priest acknowledged T.K.'s look. He too had already become suspicious that these seven men were part of the band that had attacked them at the temple. The two men began to subtly adjust their position to bracket the seven strangers between them. The Assassin, as usual, was positioned so as to be able to cover everyone in the room.

The princess and the others continued to interrogate Axe on his journey, but T.K. noted that as the men's thirst for ale became quenched a different sort of thirst became apparent in their looks at the women in the room.

"We saw signs of the beast again, or at least his handiwork at a farm—"

"A shadowbeast for certain," Chains muttered into his ale.

"Aye," Skins grinned to reveal five twisted teeth and stared hungrily at Zulla. "Some poor soul cursed by warp wizardry—like this little thing on my shoulder." He stroked the lizard skin kilt he wore. He massaged the dead creature's preserved genitals with obscene fascination. "Used to be a pretty little girl like you."

Zulla made a "yeech!" face and Skins laughed with gusto.

At that moment Jonzun and Olzen, who had been maintaining a low profile since their run in with Conkull, appeared at the top of the stairs completely unaware of the commotion down below. "So if they did walk," Jonzun was saying, "they'll need to buy a mount."

"You!" Mace snarled on seeing the two bandits at the landing.

"Oh my Akem!" Olzen exclaimed.

"You scum-bellied svor—" Knife said. "We've been after you since the temple."

"Now wait a minute, stout fellow," Olzen began, "we just—"

"We went for help!" Jonzun pleaded. "We saw poor Belijor was valiantly fighting to save us so we went to get you. But—but the vorns panicked. Ah—I take it he did not fare too well?"

"Bastard son of a tvek!" Mace spat. "And I suppose the other mounts just followed you here."

"Just so," Olzen said feebly and offered a smile.

All during this exchange the other occupants of the common room had watched with a certain premonition of dread, but it was Zul, reentering with more food that spoke up first. "Sirs, please," the innkeeper said, "there is Pax in full force in this inn. By law, you must keep your weapons and your tempers sheathed while you are at Dragonthroat."

Mace laughed a cold chilling laugh. "We don't really think too much of the law, particularly that one."

"That, sirrah, is a law of my father!" Tannilee insisted,"Not to be made light of."

"Our pardon, Madame," Axe said obsequiously, "but law has never been our strong point." On 'point,' he nodded to Knife, who drew one of his dozen blades and threw it at Jonzun. The knife struck the chubby bandit through the left bicep, eliciting a wail of pain that could have shattered glass.

"Sirrah!" Rayjol screamed. "You have violated Pax. Stop now or the imperial force will be informed." The chamberlain stepped up face to chest with Mace and attempted to stare the man down.

"Who'll tell them," Mace took his cue from Axe, "when you're pulped?" His arm swung in an arc that aimed his weighted mace right for Rayjol's head.

Ku'zn, who was standing near to the Chamberlain Rayjol reacted as fast as thought and pulled the man clear of the mace's deadly swing so that it arced onward and crushed a chair back intead of his skull.

At the same time Axe, Lance, and Skins turned to attack Shoutte. Axe was swinging his two-handed namesake, Skins a cutlass and crystal buckler, and Lance thrust a short assagi-type weapon for the priest's heart.

Shoutte threw his armful of lotion crocks in Skin's face and retreated to beyond the central fire pit. He drew Rhythemwand and maneuvered so that his back was to the pit.

T.K had been sitting opposite Sabre and beside Adriana at the next table. He was up and moving in synch with Mace's attack. He stood and pivoted, swinging his chair so that it hit Sabre as he stood.

The smallest and the quickest of the bandits, Chains, was on the earthman before he could defend himself. The whipping chain gouged a swathe across T.K.'s right arm and was on its way for a second strike when an iridescent hissing blur launched itself onto Chains, all but toppling him backwards. The man managed to get his arms up to protect his throat, but Toto's snapping and hissing kept him from doing much else.

Knife simply vaulted the fallen man and the tvek and came at T.K. He had two gleaming ten-inch daggers slashing wildly ahead of him. T.K.'s only choice was to throw himself into a backward roll over the table.

"Son-of-a-bitch!" T.K. yelled as he hit the ground beyond the table, having dropped his walking stick. He back-pedaled away from the advancing Knife and almost ran over a fleeing Orancha in the process.

"Move it or lose it, lady!" T.K. barked.

As the chair shattered under the mace Conkull picked up Tannilee with one hand and drew his greatsword with the other. He pushed his mistress behind him and ordered "Flee the room, Highness."

Then the giant was in the fray, his broadsword cleaving into the metal mace haft, locking the two weapons together. With a roar he leapt forward and bore Mace to the ground, locked as surely as their weapons.

Lord Shoutte parried and slashed with Rhythemwand as if the sword were part of him, but unlike the fight at the temple, surprise was not on his side. Despite his experience with a blade the reality of fighting multiple opponents tested his skill to the extreme.

Erique's three foes pressed him as one, the lance pricking at his legs, the axe at his head, and the cutlass at his chest. The priest's parries were all tight to his body, fractional deflections of death. There seemed no opportunity and no possibility of anything but a holding action.

"Take him now, lads," Axe commanded as he hammered yet another finger-numbing blow into the crystal sword. Suddenly Lance screamed in agony and crumpled, the tendons in the backs of his knees cut cleanly through by the two of the Assassin's crystal blades.

"Stay out of this, guildkiller," Axe cried as he and a startled Skins backed off the equally startled priest. "Your guild law says if we do not draw against you we may go unmolested."

The bandit leader moved back so that Skins, Axe, Shoutte, and the Assassin formed the corners of a square with the moaning Lance at its center.

"I am under personal contract," the Assassin said. "Yours is not the weapon to end his life. Go and leave so that…" before she could finish her statement Axe had swung his weapon in attack on her, a vertical blow she caught with crossed crystal blades.

Shoutte charged Skins and he struck his first blow with such power that the grown crystal of Rhythemwand sliced a chunk off the carved crystal of Skin's buckler.

Never a cop around when you need one! T.K. thought as he dodged another dagger slash from his opponent. Knife was cackling insanely and muttering obscenities as he slowly advanced on the limping earthman.

"Does your mother know you use words like that?" T.K. said smiling. "Do you even have a mother?" Knife growled and lunged as T.K. expected and the earthman countered by dropping forward into a leg sweep, which upended Knife and sent him sprawling. Both the dagger blades went clattering along the stone floor.

"Get the knives, Tee-Kay!" Ku'zn yelled.

For a moment T.K.'s focus went to the silvered blades and the nightmare flashed in his eyes and fixed him like a white-hot knifepoint. In that millisecond of hysterical paralysis, Sabre was upon the earthman and Mitchell had to throw himself to the left to avoid a sabre cut. He kicked hard with his right foot as he dodged and heard the satisfying crack from Sabre's right elbow.

At that same moment, Ku'zn dove for the fallen daggers, coming out of a roll with one of them just as Knife ran by on his way to T.K.

Knife whirled to face her, a curved dagger in each hand.

"I've never carved me no Z'n meat," Knife said. "I hear you hairy sluts fry up real nice." He licked his lips elaborately and waited for the image of her roasted haunch to terrify Ku'zn, but when it failed to happen he grew angry and slashed with both knives in an 'X 'pattern. The blue-furred woman howled a war cry and charged the man.

She blocked his right dagger with an outward sweep of her left hand while she pinned his left arm to his body with the dagger she carried, driving it through the arm between the ribs and into the heart. "Continentals make a better meal," Ku'zn hissed into his face as he writhed on the blade and bled his life away, "but I wouldn't feed the likes of you to a tvek."

Lord Shoutte parried a cutlass slash at his right leg, stepped in and cut upward, his crystal blade cleaving on a diagonal through the ribs and clavicle of the bandit, all but separating his head and right arm from the body.

The Assassin ducked beneath a horizontal head swipe of the axe and drove both of her blades into Axe's groin, edge upward, driving them deep and pulling them up till they exited the man's sides.

T.K. rose to his feet as Sabre transferred his weapon to his left hand and whirled it over his head to keep T.K. away. He measured the rhythm of the swing and timed his attack just as the tip passed him. He hopped in and kicked in Sabre's right kneecap with his metal foot. As the man dropped screaming, T.K. kicked once more, striking him on the temple and killing him.

The inn was suddenly quiet.

No one moved.

Less than a minute had passed since Mace had swung at Rayjol and now seven men lay dead or dying on the floor of the common room.

The smell of death, of blood, feces and bile choked the room. Conkull rolled off Mace's corpse, leaving his fingerprints imbedded in the blue white neck of the dead man. "My Princess!" he turned to an ash white Tannilee, "are you unhurt?" Then he sank to his knees, adrenalin fatigued.

Ku'zn, her fur stained a muddy purple, quickly moved to T.K.'s side to examine the wound on his arm. "This looks deep," she said with concern. "But I do not think it too bad."

T.K. smiled weakly. "Remind me not to get you angry, Peachfuzz."

She returned the smile. "You haven't seen me angry yet."

"I'll bet no one still living ever has."

Toto raised his head from Chain's savaged throat and hissed happily, moving over to T.K.'s side for a pat on the head and a "Good boy."

T.K. looked up and his eyes met Zulla's. The girl was wrapped in her father's arms. Her eyes wide with horror, but when they met T.K's they softened in concern. He smiled reassuringly to her and thought, Poor kid; this is the real stuff of nightmares.

"How fare you, Tee-Kay?" Shoutte asked from across the room. The priest stood covered in blood and gore, some of which was his own from a cut on his thigh. He had wiped Rhythemwand clean on one of the slain bandit's tunics.

"Okay," T.K. winced as Ku'zn licked his arm wound clean, "if I don't get some weird Altivan infection I'll do just fine."

"Good people," Lord Rayjol said in a calm voice that betrayed near hysteria. "Pax has been violated this day, but…" he looked gratefully at Ku'zn. "There will be no blame laid at any of you in my report for it was with clearly and truthfully the only recourse."

"We thank you all for your valiant protection," Tannilee said, affecting composure. "Come Conkull, Lord Rayjol." She turned and headed up the stairs, edging passed the sobbing Jonzun. Rayjol was right behind her followed by Conkull who, unable to free his sword from the mace haft, carried the joined weapons with him as if it was an award for valor.

"Thank you, Madame Assassin, for your timely aid." Shoutte whispered to the guild member. The black-clad woman kneeling beside the semi-conscious Lance placed a crystal blade to the man's throat and slit it from ear to ear with casual ease.

"I was trying to save you for my blade," she whispered savagely. "I have sought you too long to let some country mongrel slay you by accident."

The priest locked eyes with her then turned to fetch his medicines so that he could tend the wounded before he buried the dead.

+++

The Wizard Emperor of Mephistal stood smiling at the head of the council table in the capital city of his empire and raised his hands to silence protest. "That is a decree not subject to your baronial approval," he said in an even tone that carried to all corners of the large stone chamber as if he had yelled it. "I merely inform you out of courtesy." His smile was anything but courteous.

"But Meegana Rakkdon has served as wizard extraordinaire to the Mephon Emperors for three generations," Terack said. "To abolish her position as the official warp controller could mean disastrous price rises at warp crossings," the governor-baron of the Ell'en territory continued. "Such dealings must be regulated and overseen by a government official."

The governor-baron voiced very real fears, for Mephan was an island nation, west of both continents of Altiva and separated from the northern continent by treacherous whirlwinds that made sea trade in the north all but impossible.

"I have not abolished the position of warp controller, good gentles," Rosuff said with a smile, "I have merely assumed that position myself; this will insure the continued smooth function of all portals. As you have said,

Meegana Rakkdon has served for a long time and well at that, but—her policies have not kept pace with the needs of the Mephistal Empire. She will be pensioned and thanked appropriately for her long service." He stared down the murmur of disapproval from the Baronial Council and, when it had subsided, said beneficently, "This meeting of the council is adjourned 'til next month. Good day."

The Emperor rose and left the head of the table and as he did a tingling in the back of his skull caused him to go rigid. With a sudden painful certainty he knew that Axe, his agent on the north continent, was dead.

It is in your hands alone, My Lord Gavilon, he thought. The barrel-chested emperor's lips curled into a sneer. His sneer became a smile when he thought on what slender threads his position hung. *I will destroy your heir and then you, Meegana. When he is dead I will take great joy in watching your die slowly on the rack, I promise you.*

✦✦✦

The mushroom vaults were cold and dry yet the smell of new death made T.K. feel clammy. The exertion of carrying the bandit's bodies had coated the Earthman with sweat.

Shoutte, T.K. and Zul laid the bodies along the same wall of the cold storage room as the murdered Lady Kwa.

"Good thing I'm only passing through," T.K. leaned against a wine keg to rest. "I'm beginning to think a long stay will drive my insurance rates up."

"Healthy to jest at transitions, for it is part of the natual way of things," Shoutte knelt. "But there is no lightness in the frequency of it of late. It is far too frequent." The priest paused in saying a transition prayer for the dead bandits to study the serpent pendant around the neck of the body that had been Axe. He removed it and stood up.

"This is a wizard charm," the priest said examining the pendant closely. "Not to be disposed of lightly. Here!" He tossed it to T.K. who caught it by reflex.

✦✦✦

The Wizard Emperor suddenly knew the heir was still alive! His senses told him with no doubt that the serpent pendant was in the hand of the one he sought. Rosuff's smile became a full-throated laugh. *Of all places I wished the storm to drive him*, he thought, *He has found the most perfect place for his own death. The Goddess Shirra has honored me with great irony. I will have to sacrifice to her later at the temple.* The Wizard Emperor wore a smile the rest of the afternoon.

✦✦✦

T.K. regarded the pendant with distain. "Whoa, Erique, I'm no ghoul. I don't dig taking souvenirs from the dead. I never did it in Nam and ain't about to start."

"The dead have no use for such," Shoutte indicated Lady Kwa. "And from what I know of such things it may be useful against shadowcraft."

T.K. rolled the crystal dragon in his fingers, noting with horrific fascination that the gem figurine was warm to the touch. "Why don't you keep it then?"

"I have Rhythemwand. It is enough."

He rose to leave then paused as a thought stuck him. "Would you accompany me to the stable for a moment, Tee-Kay? I have something I wish to discuss with you." The earthman was puzzled but nodded yes, tucked the pendant into his jeans pocket and followed.

Zulla was on her hands and knees in the common room, a bucket of water beside her as she scrubbed the blood and gore off the floor. She looked up when T.K. and Shoutte entered the room and there was such fear and revulsion in her expression that T.K. stopped for a moment and gently touched her hair at the temples. She tried to smile for him and he smiled back as best he could.

Those bastards ought to burn in hell just for infecting her life with their violence, he thought.

In the stable Shoutte unrolled a long canvas package from his gear pile.

"What's the big mystery?" T.K. asked.

"No mystery," Erique whispered. "I just wished a little peace and quiet for the lesson."

"What lesson?"

Shoutte paused in his unwrapping and rose to face his companion.

"This is a sword's world, my friend, and though you may eschew its use, swords will be used against you."

For the moment the nightmare threatened to blur the earthman's vision but he forced it back into the darkness of his sleeping life where it belonged.

"I would think you've had enough proof that I can take care of myself."

"Against common ruffians, yes." Shoutte said, but continued, "The object is to successfully oppose a *skilled* opponent. In the common room, Ku'zn tells me you nearly found transition because you hesitated to gain a blade."

"I will not use a blade, Erique," T.K. eyes narrowed like a cornered animal. "That is final."

The two men faced each other and Shoutte could see by T.K.'s rigid stance that his friend was close to panic. "Be at ease, Tee-Kay. You shall not use a blade here and now—at least not against a friend." The priest bent and finished his unwrapping, drawing forth two wooden practice swords, which approximated Rhythemwand in shape. He stood and threw one of the "swords" to T.K

"No swords, Erique."

"Yes, Tee-Kay, but you must know how; it is a changing world."

"What kind of bullshit is this, Shoutte? Since when are you my guardian angel?"

"You are a stranger to this world. You do not know its ways." The priest began to circle T.K. and brought his wooden sword into a ready position.

"You saved my life at the temple after I failed to warn you; I have an obligation to see you safely on your way." T.K. remained in place, turning to keep face to face with the circling priest. He held his wooden sword casually at his right side, the tip touching the ground but his grip was a white knuckled one.

"Screw obligations, man," T.K. hissed. "I can wipe my own nose." Shoutte ignored T.K.'s remark and continued to circle him.

"There are many sword styles on this world. This is the Old Kingdom Style but one of many. The Iskarian Monk style that suits my sword Rhythemwand." Suddenly the priest sprang forward; slashing at T.K.'s head; the earthman dodged aside quickly and retreated a step.

"Stop this, Erique, before somebody gets hurt." T.K. was holding his sword with both hands now in a defensive position.

"Against the Krinarian last night, you held back," Shoutte launched a lightning quick series of cuts, which the earthman parried by the narrowest margin.

"That and your hesitation today could put your life in peril against a skilled opponent."

"I've killed a dozen men since I landed on this greaseball planet," T.K.

...THE EARTHMAN PARRIED BY THE NARROWEST OF MARGINS...

insisted, "isn't that enough for you?"

The earthman threw the wooden sword down in disgust.

"You do well for one who denies the blade."

"This is just a stick, Erique, a toy, not a blade."

"Still, you have the movements of a style. Where did you learn?"

"I studied kendo for six years before I enlisted. I never liked blades even then, but we used bamboo swords—I thought it would help me get over my fear. It didn't. And in 'Nam—" he took a deep breath and shook his head to clear away the memories. "Look, what the hell does it matter to you?"

"I like you, Tee-Kay, perhaps because you remind me of myself in my brash youth-"

"Come off it, 'grandpa', you're only a coupla years older than me."

"Or perhaps," the priest continued, "because I sense a difference about you—you are not just another warp orphan. There is the stamp of destiny on you. A quality I cannot describe." He touched Rhythemwand as if to draw knowledge from its agate handle. "I would like to see you live long enough to temper your brashness with some of the wisdom I gained through my study of the Kova."

T.K. began walking toward the inner door. "You're not going to get me to pick up a sword so stop the televangelist sermon."

Shoutte smiled softly. "A man will, on occasion, do extraordinary things to preserve his life or—"

"No lecture," T.K. said.

"My point is made," Shoutte concluded. "Altiva is a world of swords and shadowscraft—a man who commands neither is a slave to both."

T.K. paused only a second at the stable door to shoot back a look that left no doubt of his sincerity. "I like you, Erique, but you get only one warning. Pull something like this again and I swear on my mother's grave, I'll kill you."

After T.K. left Lord Shoutte picked up Rhythemwand and studied the crystal blade with intensity. "The Rhythem will be fulfilled, friend Tee-Kay," Shoutte whispered, "whether we wish it or not." Then the priest knelt to pray.

Chapter Twelve

"I hate to see a man drown, unless I'm holding him under."
Sinclair Alvin Sabre, Private Investigator

The storm continued that night with unabated fury. The mood within the inn was a dark one and so everyone retired early in hopes that sleep could blot out the memory of the afternoon's horrid violence.

Jonzun and his partner barricaded themselves in their room after the attack, refusing to come out for dinner and vowing to stay locked up until the storm was passed and they could leave the inn at a gallop.

On Rayjol's order, a deadbolt lock was added to the outside of the pair's door to make sure the two kept their word. From the songs they were singing by the time the rest of Dragonthroat retired, it was clear they had raided Zul's liquor stock as well as the larder.

The innkeeper and the madam had decided to drown their sorrows in wine and each other and were spending the night behind the locked door of his room.

Alone in her narrow bed, Zulla tossed and turned, the vivid colors of a nightmare enwrapping her like tangled sheets.

Lord Shoutte slept beside the red haired Lunit and the delicate Yomi, his crystalsword at fingertip reach above him.

The Guild Assassin sat cross-legged in her room, her ruby-crystal blades beside her. Her eyes were closed but she did not sleep. Her time sense focused forward on the moment when her husband Lee Zan Doo would be avenged.

The royal suite was also in a glum and quiet mood. Tannilee had stormed into her room, revolted by the bloody encounter she had witnessed but with too much pride to show so plebian an emotion.

Conkull slept proudly in her doorway, his great sword finally free of the mace haft (which he kept as a souvenir).

The survivors of the Kwa family slept the peaceful sleep of the drugged, while a still awake Rayjol wrote in his journal beside a single glowgem, as if afraid to lie down for fear that sleep would come and bring with it bad dreams.

On the edge of the bed Adrianna stretched her long limbs and yawned. Aside from her urgent need to empty her bladder, Adrianna of Ell'n was starving. T.K. Mitchell might be odd in many ways, but he was perfectly normal in the ones that seemed to matter, and after a bout in bed the black skinned woman always woke up ravenously hungry.

T.K. had drunk himself to sleep after athletic lovemaking and now rested comfortably beside Ku'zn, his arm thrown across the furred muscular back.

I wonder if there's any svor steak left, Adrianna thought after she relieved herself at the privy. She made her way through the quiet inn to the kitchen where she did indeed find some cooked svor flank. She ate the meat with some day old black bread she found nearby in a fresh bowl. Outside, the wind whistled a steady drone while she feasted, and she hummed a tribal lullaby her maternal aunt had taught her years ago.

Circle cast round
Blood on the ground
Summoning, dark and cold-
Cry to the night
Invoke the fright
Now as in days of old.

Hallowed the eve
For us who grieve
For our brothers and
Sisters who've passed'
The veil now is thin
And the darkness within
Is revealed in its glory at last.

I haven't thought of that song in ten years. She smiled. *I have to teach it to Lunit, she has a better voice than Aunt Thoria could ever hope to have.* She sipped some ale, enjoying the thought of her friend singing the near forgotten song.

Then she heard a noise...

+++

T.K. sensed rather than heard the door to his room ease open. He'd awakened only minutes earlier from The Nightmare and was still disoriented. When he perceived the presence in the room his first thought was, *I am under attack.*

His fingers found his walking stick and he pounced, naked, from the bed, ready to bring the cane down on the shadowed shape moving across the room.

+++

Lord Shoutte came awake with no violence, but with the sharp suddenness of a highly tuned fighter. He sat up slowly, Rhythemwand in hand.

"What is it?" A sleepy Lunit rolled over when she felt him rise, but didn't open her eyes. "Is something wrong?"

"No," Shoutte whispered, staring at the Assassin, who stood waiting in the doorway. "Go back to sleep, little waterbird. I'll be back presently." Lunit mumbled and rolled back over.

The Assassin waited patiently while the priest dressed in breechclout, low boots, and a short blue robe embroidered along the shoulders with the feathered serpent that was his family crest. He carried the scabbarded Rhythemwand with a relaxed grip. "I am ready."

+++

"Jeez, Pumpkin." T.K. said as he barely avoided clubbing Zulla unconscious. "You could have gotten yourself killed, sneaking up like that."

The terrified girl was frozen in place, stunned into speechlessness by the near miss. She stared at the naked apparition towering above her with the eyes of a trapped doe and began to quietly cry.

"Easy, sweetie," he murmured, setting the stick on a table. "You just scared the daylights out of me. That's all."

A low growl from the bed drew both their attentions to Ku'zn, who was crouching beside the bed, hands curled into claws. Her fur was standing on end and her long hair exploded in tangles from her head.

Tiny Zulla threw herself forward into T.K.'s arms and exclaimed "Oh, my!" with such melodramatic furor that T.K. gently laughed.

"It's okay, Pumpkin, she's a teddy bear, when she's awake anyway." He noticed that Ku'zn's eyes were unfocused and glazed over.

"Ku'zn," he called out with concern, "Peachfuzz, it's me, T.K." He was greatly relieved when he saw the blue-furred woman blink and relax as she came fully awake.

"Hi there, fuzzy, welcome back." He smiled at the puzzled Z'n. "Glad you made it back from Dozeland," T.K. said. "I knew a G.I. once who busted up his wife's whole family before they woke him up from a flashback nightmare. He was real contrite."

"I didn't mean to cause so much trouble for you," Zulla whined pitifully. "I'm sorry I just—I uh—I couldn't sleep and I wanted to talk to you Tee-Kay." She began to sob again. "I'll go away."

Ku'zn was quick to realize what was happening and picked up her dress. "I see Adrianna's gone, probably to fill her belly. She usually does after she's filled her—"

"Ku'zn!" T.K. cut her off sharply and made an embarrassed face. Ku'zn smiled as she walked past.

"You're very cute being shy when you're dressed like that," the Z'n quipped, then was gone out the doorway. T.K. realized he was naked and jumped away from the teenager, turning his back to slip into his blue jeans.

"Don't be silly, Zulla," he said at last, a little composed. He sat down on the edge of the bed so he could look her more directly in the eyes. "Tell me what's wrong, kiddo." The teenager looked around, uncertain whether to stay or go, but her need to be comforted won out over her embarrassment and she climbed onto T.K.'s lap.

"I had another bad dream," she said, absorbed in his brown eyes, "about all those men that were killed before." She squeezed her eyes shut to hold out the memory.

"I know, honey," T.K. said.

He wrapped his arms around her and pulled her close to him. She returned the gesture, enjoying the muscular shoulders her arms could barely reach around and the salty smell of his skin.

"Images like today," he said, "I know they burn themselves into you, Pumpkin, like a brand. They don't really go away, cause they really happened, but you can deal with it. All you can do is try and paint them over with good memories."

He fought back his onw nightmare's crimson images and thought, *Hypocrite.*

"I'll try, Tee-Kay," she smiled weakly. "I have good memories of you now." Without warning she kissed him quickly on the cheek and then snuggled her head into the hollow of his neck to forestall any reprimand.

T.K. blushed and felt himself ashamed at enjoying the physical contact and wondered what he felt for the nubile teen. This better get me nominated for sainthood, he thought, *or at least take a couple of notches off my debt sheet.*

"Can I stay with you for tonight, Tee-Kay?" she said softly into his shoulder. "I won't bother you or the fuzzy lady or nothing; I just don't want to be alone with my dreams."

"Sure, Pumpkin," he whispered to the top of her head. "I know what you mean."

✦✦✦

"This letter is written in Mephan, Orian and Umbrian," Shoutte whispered. "I have signed it so that there can be no doubt of my intent."

He set the tvek-hide scroll on a bale of the supplies by the wagon. The inquisitive Toto, who had been consigned to sleeping in the barn for becoming too interested in T.K.'s sex life, trotted over to sniff at the scroll.

"Here is my letter," the Assassin said, placing hers beside Shoutte's, "written in Mephan; it is the only writing I know." She stepped away, her eyes never leaving Shoutte's.

"The letter will absolve you of any wrongdoing in breaking Pax with me," Shoutte spoke quietly.

"As will mine," she said, adding, "Shall we begin?" She drew her two blades and stepped back into a crouch.

"A moment please," Shoutte said. He went to the stable door and swung it open. "Here, boy, come." He waived Toto to his side and ushered the curious lizard into the common room with a gentle nudge.

"Wise," the Assassin said. "Most will ignore the vorns' bleatings if they hear; the tvek's screech they would investigate." Shoutte closed the door and leaned a barrel against it.

"One last request if you will," the priest said as he drew Rhythemwand and set aside the scabbard. "What is the name of the person whom I fight?"

"I am Lee Zan Kar," the woman said with pride removing her hood to reveal a face that was younger than most would have supposed from her manner. Only her eyes seemed older and burned with the fire of vengeance. "I am the wife of Lee Zan Doo, for whom I do this." She tossed the hood aside and resumed her defensive crouch.

Since both were using crystal blades neither combatant bothered with body armor. Only grown crystal armor would be effective defense against grown crystal blades and very few in the world had such protection. Steel or carved crystal armor might deflect a grown crystal blow, but in the case of this fight to the death it would only delay the outcome. Better the speed of the unencumbered body than the weight of the marginally useful armor.

"I am Erique, Shoutte of Shoutte, priest of the Kova. I meet you in fair combat, with no reservation. Let the Rhythem be fulfilled, Lee Zan Kar,"

Lord Shoutte said moving into a middle guard with his crystal blade. "We begin."

+++

Ku'zn came down the stairs still smiling at T.K.'s embarrassment. The common room was empty and quiet save for the constant howl of the wind from the skylight. It was a sound the blue furred woman found oddly comforting. It reminded her of her windswept homeland, the island of Z'n S'a in the oceans to the west of the contintent.

"Oh, Windmother," she prayed as she stopped beneath the skylight to gaze up at the fury of the storm. "Carry my thoughts to my brother and our homeland to—" She stopped. There was a movement near the shadowed corner of the room.

The Z'n woman fell into a crouch, baring fang-like incisors and growling deep in her throat. "Face me, or die," she called out.

Toto padded sleepily into the light.

"Oh," Ku'zn said with a smile of relief. "Hello fearsome beast."

The tvek inclined his head and walked over to a few feet from the woman to pause and sniff. "Oh, I see," she said, "I have it wrong; I'm the fearsome beast. Well, it is good to be cautious; come along." She patted her hip then turned toward the kitchen.

Toto followed.

At the threshold of the room both woman and tvek halted with ears prickled and nostrils flared. There was the fresh smell of death in the kitchen. Recent and bloody.

The tvek froze at the doorway, razor beak clicking. Ku'zn moved forward at a crouch all senses alert for attack. Then she saw something near the center table.

+++

T.K. finally dozed off in an upright position with his back to the headboard of the bed. Zulla lay quietly asleep in his lap. Suddenly a wail of agony unlike any he had ever heard pulled the earthman back to full wakefulness. "Holy spit!" he exclaimed as he all but threw Zulla to the bed and rose to grope for his moccasins.

"What is it?" Zulla asked with renewed terror.

"Unless I'm wrong it's more freakin' trouble—I think that sound was

Ku'zn!" He had slipped the shoes on his feet and raced out the door holding his walking stick and a shirt before Zulla could slide off the bed and follow.

In the stable Lord Shoutte was parrying a belly swipe from one of the Assassin's crystal blades when the banshee wail tore through the inn. He finished his parry, but instead of riposting, he leapt back into *en guarde*.

"Truce?" Shoutte whispered.

The Assassin looked frustrated but nodded. Shoutte waited for her to lower her swords before he turned and unbarred the door.

"Curse it to the ephemeral pits," the woman swore, throwing her blades to the ground with a clatter. "Will there never be an end to this?"

The minute it took Shoutte to unbar the door to the stable allowed T.K. to reach the spiral stairs so that both men met in the center of the common room.

"Kitchen!" Shoutte whispered and the two of them altered course.

At the door to the shadowed kitchen they stopped. Adrianna lay sprawled on the kitchen floor, her throat ripped all but completely through, and a drying pool of blood spread around her like an open flower. Kneeling in the pool of blood and tearing at her own fur so that it came out in handfuls was Ku'zn. Toto paced nervously behind the Z'n, hissing and clicking in his own animal cry of anguish.

"Aw, hell!" T.K. felt his knees go weak as he looked at the remains of the woman he had made love to only hours before. His stomach began to heave and he tasted bile, but he choked it back and moved over beside Ku'zn.

The Z'n almost stuck out at him when T.K. touched her shoulder, but then she wrapped herself around him and sobbed, swept up in her grief.

The doorway began to fill with the occupants of the inn but all were unnaturally quiet, even Lunit and Yomi who pushed through to kneel and join their contract sister in her pain.

Finally tiny Zulla broke through her own shock enough to ask, "Where is my father?" She ran across the kitchen to the heavy door of Zul's room and tried the handle. The door was locked, so she reached over to a small pull cord on the wall, which rang a bell they could distantly hear from the other side of the door. She pulled three times in a signal.

"Oh father, please be all right!" she said, "Why did you have to have such a heavy door?" She pulled on the chord again. This time she was rewarded when the door swung in to reveal Zul and Orancha.

"What's all this racket?" a drunk Orancha said, slurring her r's. Then she saw Adrianna's ravaged body and hurled herself down at it. Lunit and

Yomi caught her as a new round of hysterics began from all four of them.

"Are you alright, daughter?" Zul asked as he surveyed the carnage.

"Yes, father," she answered, "I was with T.K. when we heard the scream." Zul was a little startled at that and his look to T.K. seemed all too familiar to the earthman.

Oh God, T.K. thought distancing himself from Ku'zn's grief and his own pain. *Just what I need now, another irate relative and when I'm actually innocent this time.*

Tannilee chose that moment to arrive and catch her first sight of the body. "By the lady's veil!" the Princess exclaimed as she saw the mess. Then her royal nerves gave out as her knees buckled and she fainted. Lord Shoutte caught her.

"Okay, everybody," T.K. said in his best imitation D.I. voice. "Let's all go out into the main room. Now!"

Lord Shoutte and Tannilee were already in the common room and her party followed. T.K. took Ku'zn by her shoulders and helped her to her feet.

"Come on, Peachfuzz," he said gently, "Let's mourn after we figure this all out." He stared into her unfocused eyes until she could see him and then added, "We need you back here, babe. Don't take a twister home on me."

"I'm alright now, Tee-Kay," The Z'n said, her voice still a little gravelly from her yell. "What must be done?"

"Let's get Madame and the others into the common room and count heads. I think it's the same animal, that freaking shadowbeast."

It took five minutes to settle everyone down in the main room. Zul served wine and everyone tried to focus his or herself again to deal with this new horror.

"It's that creature again," T.K. said as he belted back his second cup of wine. "Those marks were exactly the same as Lady Kwa."

"And Beokta and the children." Shoutte whispered bitterly. T.K. Shoutte, the Assassin, and Lord Rayjol were sequestered at a table by the kitchen door. "It somehow has gained reentry to the inn," Shoutte said.

"Or never left at all," the Assassin said.

"Meaning?" T.K. asked.

"It has some place of concealment we did not discover."

"Or perhaps a hidden or secret doorway?" Lord Rayjol said.

"Anyway it works out," T.K. said, "It's a fair bet that if we didn't find it the first time we'd be wasting our time with a second search. Agreed?" The others at the table nodded in agreement.

"Then what do we do?" the Princess Tannilee stepped up to the table, followed closely by Conkull. Lord Rayjol began to rise to offer her his seat but she stayed him with a gesture. "I am too restless to sit. Please continue your discussion." She was obviously still shaken by the sight of Adrianna's corpse.

"Way ah see it," T.K. said with an added western twang. "We just circle the wagons and make camp here." When everyone looked at him oddly, he explained. "We just sit tight here in the common room all together until the storm is over. Strength in numbers and all that."

"Safe, the herd—alone is death," Tannilee said, obviously quoting an old folk saying. She gave a half-smile that T.K. returned.

"A sensible idea," Lord Rayjol said. "We certainly have food and drink enough."

"The nerves of these people will not endure a long wait," the Assassin said ominously.

"A good point," T.K. said. "I'm not sure I'm up to it myself, but what other choice do we have?"

"And our two little thieves have not yet ventured forth," Lord Shoutte said. "They should be warned as well. Even they have a better end due them then to blunder blindly into this monster. I suggest that I rouse them, retrieve my medicines, and make a cursory search on my way back. We can at least reclaim the upper floor."

"We must find this beast and destroy it, my lord Priest," Tannilee said, "but no more should be risked unnecessarily. You must be accompanied."

"As you say, Highness," Lord Shoutte acquiesced. "But the main force of arms should stay down here with those who need the protection most."

"I will accompany you, noble priest," Lee Zan Kar, the Assassin, said in a sweet voice.

"Many thanks, guild sister," Shoutte said with a humor which made T.K. look at him questioningly.

"Where a sword arm may be missed," the princess said as the two men prepared to rise, "an extra pair of eyes will be best used in defense. Lord Rayjol, accompany Lord Shoutte and this lady." The Chamberlain looked as if he might faint in fear but he surprised it beneath centuries of breeding and nodded yes.

"May the Rhythem be fulfilled, friends," Lord Shoutte said as he started for the stairs.

"Watch your own back, Buddy," T.K. said quietly to Lord Shoutte as he walked him to the stairs. "I'm not so sure Bozo and his mate will be any help."

"Rest assured, Tee-Kay," Shoutte said. "We will be back."

"Be careful, Tee-Kay," Zulla said materializing at the earthman's side.

"I'm staying with you, Pumpkin," he said. "I'm a devout practicing coward." He put his arm around her and squeezed as they watched the three people ascend the stairs.

Lord Shoutte led the three, Rhythemwand drawn and held out in challenge like a beacon. Rayjol came next and the Assassin followed. Even the chamberlain seemed to hope they would meet and kill the shadowbeast and put an end to the fear. They moved straight to the bandits' room and Lord Shoutte removed the outer bar from the door.

"Please come out, gentlemen," Lord Rayjol commanded. "There has been another murder and we are all assembling in the common room." There was no answer from within and Lord Rayjol called out again. "This is a royal decree for your own safety. Open the door."

Still no reply.

Lord Shoutte pounded on the door with the pommel of Rhythemwand and Rayjol asked once more for the men to unbar the door but there was still no sound from inside the room.

"Stand back," Shoutte whispered, raised his crystalsword and, after a moment's hesitation, sliced the blade down into the door with a mighty heave. Wood splintered.

The blade sank deeply into the door and Shoutte had to work the sword free. Four more strokes separated the inner bar and the splintered door exploded inward.

Shoutte stepped inside with the others right behind and they all halted at the horrific sight before them.

"By the lady's veil," Lord Rayjol said, "It will never end."

+++

"I don't like this," T.K. said, his eyes riveted on the stairs. "They're taking too long." He rose from his seat intent on going after the others but Zulla's urgent voice checked him.

"Don't go Tee-Kay, they'll be alright." Her doe eyes were pleading.

"You're probably right, Pumpkin," he said sitting down. "That monster is more than likely back in hiding somewhere down here or outside."

"Damn!" he said suddenly bending down to scratch at where the ankle brace entered his moccasin. "Damn itch!"

A curious and edgy Toto nosed at the earthman's scratching fingers and T.K. gave him a quick pet on the beak.

"Does it hurt much?" Zulla asked with concern.

"No, honey, it's just what they call phantom itch. The nerve endings sort of remember the whole foot—-when I'm tired or nervous mostly. Both of which I am now."

The teenager looked at the metal brace intensely and summoned up her courage to ask. "Did it hurt much when you had your accident?"

T.K. looked at her and smiled ruefully. "Yeah, but more inside than out. I felt a lot more than nerve endings die; that's when I realized people are nothing but savages inside. Bloodthirsty unfeeling savages. I knew then how much innocents suffer at the hands of us—warriors. Ha!"

He was crying quite suddenly, excess emotion distilling from his fear and anxiety and self-pity, spilling out on him unwished for and uncontrolled. He had to speak of it or it would explode within him. He was only vaguely aware of Zulla's arms around his shoulders.

"Vietnam was like a bad hit of acid that just wouldn't go away," he said slowly, as if the power of speech were a new discovery. "Every color and sound was more intense and you just knew every minute that it could be your last. You became certain it would be your last. And when someone around you bought the farm you wondered why you hadn't. It did that to your way of thinking." His eyes were focused in the past and he was hidden inside the bunker of his mind, watching and for the first time not actually feeling The Nightmare. His voice became strangely calm.

"I knew these two Republic of Korea marines, Cho and Kim. We were stationed in Saigon and got to be good drinking buddies. Good friends. We were into the martial arts and would workout together. They both had long hair, you know. The brass let the ROK Marines get away with that stuff and a lot of other things 'cause they were such kick ass soldiers." He laughed sardonically and Zulla hugged him more tightly, feeling the waves of pain coming off him.

"And they were, too." He continued, "Real old time Sulsa warriors. Iron men with steel nerves, that sort of thing. Saved my pink hairless butt a couple of times, in bar fights and out in the green."

"We were like brothers, you know. And they dug my Filipino style. We were sort of the Three Musketeers, with this engineer Locke as our D'artagnon."

He forced his voice out through a throat choked with emotion. "Then we were on this S.O.G. incursion and we three went out as point scouts. Some kid, I never knew if it was a boy or girl—maybe eight or nine years old, comes out of the undergrowth with this big old French bayonet like a freakin' short sword, and tries to stab Kim." He could see the images of his memory before him as if it were film projected. He felt oddly detached from it yet he shivered as if a sudden chill.

"Just a kid, but that's what it was like, you know. Kim gave the kid a rifle butt in the face and knocked him down. Cho grabbed the bayonet. He stepped up to the kid, laughing and started to disembowel the kid with the knife. The kid was screaming and Kim smashed his mouth in with the gun butt. Blood and teeth and this horrible gurgling sound. And the knife cutting."

"I went berserk. I blew Kim's head off. Cho turned and threw the knife at me, shooting as he did. All I saw, though, was the knife coming straight at me, turning end over end. He shot my foot to hell. I killed him, I blew his head off."

T.K. became aware of Zulla staring at him, herself near tears, her expression one of frozen horror. To her he said softly, "I drank with them, whored with them, in every way I was just like them, even when I killed them."

"You killed…" she said, not wanting to believe his story.

"I'm an evil man, Pumpkin. I've killed to stay alive, out of fear and out of rage. But that once I killed because it made me feel good. It made me feel cleaner to kill them."

He was suddenly aware of the girl's arms around him and the fact that she was shivering. He tried to smile. "You have a talent for getting to the heart of me, Pumpkin. I've never told that story to anyone. Not the doctors or the shrinks at the V.A. Even the War Department thinks we triggered an ambush. I got a freakin' Purple Heart out of it." He made no attempt to leave her embrace.

"You're not evil, Tee-Kay," Zulla said with absolute belief. "You're a good man. I wish I could take the nightmares away from you so you could see it." T.K. leaned forward and kissed the teenager tenderly on the cheek.

"You help me see a little, Pumpkin."

The girl blushed. "I… uh…like you a lot, Tee-Kay."

"I like you too, Zulla."

"You keep your hands to yourself, Warp Orphan," the innkeeper said, grabbing Zulla by the arm and pulling her to her feet. "And as for you," he snarled at his daughter, "I will not accept such brazen behavior from a child of mine."

"I'm not a suckling babe to be dictated to," the embarrassed and enraged teenager yelled at her father. "Let me have my life." She burst into tears and ran off into the kitchen.

"You're the cause of this!" Zul hissed at T.K. "Filling her head with..."

"Just cut the cliché speech, Pop," the earthman said with barely contained emotion. "Chill out. There's no reason to upset her more or piss me off. I'm not a good person to piss off especially right now. That kid needs your understanding, not your rightous rage." T.K. was on his feet now, facing off with the father, neither man willing to make an emotional compromise.

"Go tend your daughter with a gentle hand," Ku'zn said, stepping between the two men, "and you, Tee-Kay can comfort me, I am frightened."

The two men stared at each other for a second longer and then Zul turned with a grumbled curse and went off after Zulla.

T.K. watched him go and then looked at Ku'zn and laughed.

"Frightened, Fuzzball? I think I love you." He threw his arms around her and they hugged.

"I heard your tale," she said softly.

"I made a public spectacle of myself, huh?"

"No," she said, "I have big ears. I did not know many of the words, but it will help that I understand some now. My people believe that an evil dream has power only in the darkness and that there is no greater darkness than one's silence and loneliness."

"I always used to sleep through philosophy class," T.K. quipped. "Come on, let's go get tanked." He smiled without too much effort and she nodded.

They turned their backs to the stairs not noticing the section of the wall that soundlessly slide aside to reveal a dark figure within.

Chapter Thirteen

"Someday I'm gonna get me a female dog and name her Payback, just because."
T.K. Mitchell

T.K. and Ku'zn both whirled around, ready to fight at the sound of a boot sole scrapping against the stone floor. The earthman snapped his cane at the shadow figure as it came from the opening but the cane was parried with a crystalline ting.

"Oh crap, Erique," T.K. moaned. "Does everybody on this planet sneak up on everybody else? Where does that go?"

The Assassin stepped through the narrow opening after Shoutte and paused to help Lord Rayjol through. "This is but one passage, which leads from the room of those two unfortunates," Lord Rayjol said.

"O and J?" T.K. asked. "What's up with them?"

"Slaughtered like svor," Shoutte said, sheathing his sword.

"The shadowbeast?" Ku'zn asked.

"Yes," the Assassin said, her gaze drifting across the room to focus on Zul. "But a shadowbeast it would seem who has intimate knowledge of this and perhaps other secret passages."

All eyes turned to the startled innkeeper but no one could find words until his daughter spoke. "What does she mean, father?"

Zul spared only a moment to regard Zulla with an agonized look before he bolted for the kitchen. Shoutte and the Assassin both raced after him with T.K. limping behind. But the innkeeper was through the door and into the cellar before anyone could reach him.

"He's barred the other side," the Assassin said after a futile attempt to open the heavy door.

"Cut through it with your crystal sword," Rayjol commanded of Shoutte.

"It will take much longer than the other door," Shoutte said. "Too long. Better to block this side and go down through the passageway."

"He mustn't escape," Tannilee insisted.

"Where can he go in the Z'last?" Ku'zn observed.

"Where could those guys come from?" T.K. asked, fingering the serpent pendant. "Don't take anything for granted."

"What's going on?" a crying Zulla demanded. "Why did father run away?"

T.K. went to the teenager and slipped an arm around her while Ku'zn discreetly herded the others back into the common room.

"Easy, Pumpkin," T.K. said, "maybe he was scared too."

"Don't hurt him. He's all I have." Her words were forced out between wracking sobs. The earthman stroked her hair to calm her and found himself enjoying the silky texture.

"I'll bring him back okay, Pumpkin," he whispered. "I'll make it all right. I promise."

T.K. led the girl back to the common room to find that Shoutte, the Assassin, and Ku'zn had already entered the secret passage in search of Zul.

"Stay with Lunit, Zulla," T.K. said, turning the girl over to the red-haired woman. "I've got to go too."

Toto nudged up to Zulla, hissed affectionately, and licked the back of

"HE'S BARRED THE OTHER SIDE."

her hand. "You stay with her Toto, boy," T.K. said, "she'll protect you." The tvek hissed as if it understood and sat at the girl's feet.

"Be careful, warp orphan," Lunit called after him. She helped the young girl over to a table where Orancha was sitting with a stunned expression.

The secret passage was cool and damp and faintly lit by widely spaced glowgems set along the walls. *Okay, guys*, T.K. thought, *which way did you go?*

He listened intently and heard muffled conversation off to his right. He began to walk slowly in the direction of the sound.

A few minutes further on he called out softly "Erique! Peachfuzz!" and was rewarded with a loud "Shh!" from around a turn.

"Why didn't you stay with the others?" Shoutte whispered as they proceeded.

"Hello to you, too. I have a promise to keep, if you must know."

"There," Shoutte said, pointing. "Those are the stairs that lead down." The four searchers, with Shoutte in the lead, followed the rough-hewn steps down until they ended on the floor of the mushroom vault.

"Look at this," Ku'zn drew their attention to a heavy wooden steel-banded door set solidly into the rock of the cavern wall. Across the door was a broad steel bar with a crystal bolt securely fastened to it.

"Something of value within, perhaps?" the blue-furred woman suggested.

"But why no lock, only a bar and bolt," the Assassin mused, "unless to keep something on the other side?"

T.K. stepped forward, unbarred the door, and pulled it open. "It's a cell!" the earthman said. Inside the room was a bare ten-foot cube carved out of the solid rock, with neither bench nor other furniture to provide comfort. On careful examination no secret panel could be discerned.

"It does appear to be a cell or cage," Lord Shoutte agreed. The four stood inside the strange room and stared at the walls, which like the inside of the door, were covered with hundreds of scratches.

"Like some crazed animal had been locked in here," Ku'zn murmured, "or a shadowbeast."

"Zul's got a lot to explain when we catch his ass," T.K. said as they exited the room.

"Our search should be systematic," Lord Shoutte suggested. "Rhythemwand will protect me; you three go down tha—" Suddenly the piercing siren of Tannilee's scream cut through the vaulted caverns and froze the four of them in place.

"The common room!" Shoutte said as he raced toward the secret passageway. They could only move in single file up the hidden corridor with Lord Shoutte, the Assassin, Ku'zn, and lastly T.K. racing as fast as they could. They moved with a single purpose, scraping and bumping against the irregular walls with no regard for themselves.

The screams grew more frantic with terror as they got closer to their point of entry and it became easier for the four runners to distinguish roars and growls amongst the screams.

Finally they reached the passage entrance and burst through into the bloody hell that the common room had become.

✛✛✛

The Wizard Emperor Roosuf cleared his throat to call the reconvened council of barons to attention. He then basked in the sudden quiet of their focus. "It is simple enough news to absorb, good gentles," the wizard emperor said calmly. "I have received word that a distant relative of the old Emperor Kantos is dead in Cosen. That is where my Lord Gavilon has been dispatched to retrieve the body, so we may give it the ceremony it is due."

"But how is that we never heard of this distant relative?" Duke Havros asked from the foot of the table. "And just how did this child of Sphona die?"

"Did I say he was a child of Sphona's?" Roosuf asked with a reptile smile. His smile quickly faded into a false look of concern. "A wild beast I believe. Tragic."

"Yes," Baron Kostan murmured, "tragic, especially coming so soon after the discovery of the possible heir's existence."

"True," Roosuf said, "but we cannot all account for the dice of the fates." At the head of the table the Wizard Emperor smiled and left to begin making arrangements for a magnificent state funeral for the newly departed heir.

"He was our only chance of raising the people," Duke Havros whispered to Meegana. "With him gone it will take a long time and much luck to unseat Roosuf."

"He is guessing," Meegana replied. "He has to be. The warp ports to Cosen have not been aligned, that he might know for certain."

"The council must know—" Havros said with more urgency then the wizardess had heard from him before. "I must know."

"I will leave soon," Meegana said. "There are a few tricks of the craft that even Roosuf does not know. I will bring back the heir or proof that he is dead."

✦✦✦

T.K. was the last one through the door into the common room. It was like he had stepped into his own nightmare and brought everyone at the inn with him.

The room was a portrait painted in blood: Tannilee and the survivors of the Kwa family were huddled behind an overturned table. Lunit and Yomi, with chairs held in their hands like shields, were backed against the far wall, with Toto lying bloodied and moaning at their feet. An explosion of blood high up on the wall cascaded down to cover the two escorts and half the room, pooling on the floor.

Madame Orancha, Rayjol, and the mighty and bleeding Conkull, each holding weapons, were clustered in a half circle in the center of the room surrounding the painter of the grisly portrait: the shadowbeast.

It was not as big as T.K. thought it should be, but it was as fierce and crazed as a shark and every bit the image of the violence it had wrought.

No taller than Orancha, it stood upright on hind legs and had two almost human arms. Its head joined its body on a surprisingly thin neck and was graced with two large red eyes and a wide, fleshy-lipped mouth which when opened revealed razor fangs in abundance. The creature was a mottled grey-blue and covered with tiny bumps that made it look sickly and misshapen.

As the earthman watched, the creature darted forward at blinding speed and raked a taloned hand across Orancha's throat, all but decapitating her.

Conkull leapt in with his great two-handed sword and struck a solid blow to the creature's back, but the steel blade clanged without effect against the knobby skin. The blow enraged the beast, which spun on the Krinarian and, with a single backhand swipe of its arm, sent Conkull flying against the wall.

It was then that T.K. saw that the creature's skin was indeed shark-like, for the knobs which covered it were razor sharp and even the contact of the hand had slashed the barbarian bloody.

"Assassin, quickly," Lord Shoutte commanded as he raced forward. Lee Zan Kar obeyed without a word, drawing her ruby blades and racing to outflank the creature.

Priest and Assassin moved in on the beast while the Chamberlain ran to the aid of the fallen Conkull.

The creature seemed to sense that the nature of its opponents and their weapons were different for it regarded them with wary eyes, its breath coming in staccato pants. The two crystalsword-holders began to walk the creature back toward the kitchen with slow steady steps.

Ku'zn and T.K. crossed the room to where Orancha had fallen, joined by Lunit and Yomi, but the madame was clearly beyond any help. The earthman ran from there to Toto and found the tvek to be alive but in great pain, its side ripped open and some of the old wounds re-bloodied.

"Easy boy," T.K. whispered. "I'll take care of you."

A growling Ku'zn took her place beside the Assassin, to be joined by a staggering and sanguine Conkull, Rayjol, and Lunit. The shadowbeast moved back steadily toward the kitchen, perplexed by the first concerted opposition it had ever faced.

A horrible thought occurred to T.K. as he frantically surveyed the room. "Where's Zulla?" he asked Yomi.

"I do not know," the tiny, almond-eyed woman said, her eyes locked on the remains of Orancha. "The shadowbeast just seemed to come out of nowhere. I didn't see what happened to her."

The earthman stood and looked around; hoping to see the girl huddled behind an overturned table but there was no sign of her. At that moment, near the kitchen door the shadowbeast loosened a howl of confined rage. It cut through the constant wail of the Z'last and through the soul of every person in the inn, freezing them.

The cry abruptly stopped and the creature rushed forward, seizing Rayjol by the face and yanking him into the air with an audible crack. The creature hurled him directly into Conkull and Ku'zn, knocking the two of them down. Gore sprayed everywhere from Lord Rayjol's crushed skull.

The shadowbeast attempted to push through the break in the circle but the Assassin leapt in front of it, and slashed twice with her ruby blades. The creature howled in pain as the blades left bloody rents in its armor-like skin and clubbed the woman to the ground with its fists.

The creature then crouched to finish the dazed woman with its talons, but it was stopped by Lord Shoutte with Rhythemwand, who literally jumped to straddle the Assassin, and slash at the creature.

The beast's rage trebled. It seized the hilt of Rhythemwand as Shoutte completed the arc of a cut and ripped the sword from the priest's hands, hurling the blade past him toward T.K.

The earthman watched the crystalsword clatter to the floor with the fascination that a man falling from a great height watches the ground.

The whole room suddenly crossed from horrific reality into nightmare. Everything was suddenly dream speed, neither fast nor slow, but with every movement in the room painfully studied.

The giant Conkull cradled the bloody Rayjol in his arms and cried like a child. The downed Assassin scrambled in frantic slow motion to get out from below Lord Shoutte to use her weapons, while the shadowbeast raked razor claws across Shoutte's stomach in a spray of red.

With the acute reality of the waking nightmare T.K. watched the crystal blade at his feet become the bloody bayonet, Lord Shoutte, the child, and the beast became his friend, Duk. He knew what he must do. He had to pick up the blade.

The blade.

The bloody blade.

Oh God, T.K. thought, *I can't do it.* His hand was frozen as he reached for the serpent handle, his fingers only inches from the cool agate.

He looked up and saw the child, covered with gore, driving his open hand into the creature's face in a futile effort to defend himself.

And the sounds of the M16 got louder and closer.

And Duk screamed.

And the creature screamed as T.K. slashed Rhythemwand across its side. Then the earthman lunged as the shadowbeast turned from the bleeding priest, driving the crystal blade into the shoulder of the monster. The shadowbeast screamed again and ran screaming into the kitchen.

"Follow it!" Lord Shoutte gasped as he fell to his knees. "It must be stopped."

The Assassin raced by and the earthman followed at a run, aware as in a dream that Ku'zn was at his side.

The shadowbeast had left the kitchen, leaving a clear trail in blood to the secret passage it had used. "Quickly!" the Assassin yelled as she raced into the passage with T.K. behind her.

This is not happening, T.K. thought, *I am not on a search and destroy, holding a machete in my hand and covered with somebody else's gore. Not again.*

"There!" The Assassin moved through a doorway to the right where the howl of the storm seemed louder. A moment later there was a snarl and she flew backward into the corridor to strike against the rear wall. T.K. stepped over the Assassin with the sword that felt so strange held out before him.

The doorway led to a dead end. In the dead end the shadowbeast stood its back toward him, apparently intent on something on the wall.

"This is it you motherfu—" T.K. said as he thrust with Rhythemwand, but before the blade struck the beast the wall behind it slid aside and the monster ran headlong out into the howling fury of the storm.

"Damn!" T.K. ran forward after the creature, barely aware of the biting cold, the wind that whipped him or the shout from Ku'zn saying, "You'll be killed!" All he was aware of was the shadowbeast running ahead of him.

The winds were hurricane force and the temperature below freezing. It was pitch dark but T.K. moved forward, untroubled by no more than a stiff autumn breeze. He felt the wizard charm against his chest glow a warm blue and realized it was why he did not feel the Z'last.

Profitable for grave robbing, he allowed himself to think, but it doesn't do squat for visibility.

He stood still trying to find the monster but sand and airborne debris made vision beyond a few inches impossible. Even the cave mouth he had come from was lost in the murk.

"Damn son of a bit—" Suddenly the shadowbeast was on him, flying out of the darkness and slamming into the earthman, knocking him off his feet and cutting off his breath.

The two rolled down the slope of the mountain for a dozen feet, locked together, the rough, sharp hide of the creature lacerating the earthman who had Rhythemwand wedged between them. They smashed into an outcropping of rock and the creature was thrown clear. T.K. scrambled to his feet, desperately trying to get his bearings and drew the sword up in front of him.

We're standing on the skylight of the inn, T.K. realized. The light around him was coming from below. His knees felt weak.

The monster reared up in front of T.K., its strange eyes burning, its mouth twisted in a snarl with *pain. Its taloned hands thrust out for his throat.*

You're not gonna kill any more kids, Duk. T.K. thought. *I can't let you.*

The shadowbeast charged; a phantom M16 fired.

The crystal sword leapt forward at the armored chest.

There was a scream.

+++

Lord Erique Shoutte was losing a lot of blood and Lunit was bending over him, naked, using her dress as a great bandage around his torn abdomen. The adrenalin rush had subsided and the pain was so intense he wavered on the edge of consciousness.

He was nodding out when a sudden, brilliant flash of agony passed through him and he knew the agony was not his; it was the shadowbeast's! He felt it through Rhythemwand.

"By the pit, no!" he whispered to himself with a sudden horrific realization that pain brought him.

There was an explosion above the room. Lightning arced through the skylight, the thick crystal panes shattering into a rain of splinters.

"Cover your faces!" Lunit screamed, throwing herself over the priest, only be covered to in turn by Conkull.

Two bodies fell through the crystal shower; one skewered through the center and too weak from agony to even scream; the other, a frantic whirlwind, clutching for survival.

One of the whirlwind's bloody hands grabbed a solid hold of a scale on the dragon chimney and slammed against it with a cry of pain. He hung there moaning while the dying body slammed to the floor with a horrible thud.

T.K. was suspended by a wrenched right arm. The blinding pain finally subsided enough for him to think clearly. *Gotta get down.* He snaked his legs around the dragon and climbed down slowly.

The winds of the Z'last were starting to fill the common room. The survivors wasted no time in dragging the wounded and then the dead into the kitchen, improvising a door with a turned over table.

T.K. helped Lunit drag Shoutte to safety, then collapsed beside the priest.

"Let me pick the next hotel, Erique," T.K. quipped with no humor in his tone. "I don't care if it has a hot tub either."

Everyone was in shock.

The only sounds in the room were moans and rasped breaths.

Ku'zn and the Assassin re-entered, ready to tell all that T.K. had been swallowed by the Z'last falling silent when they saw the carnage.

"My friend," Lord Shoutte whispered weakly, "please bring me Rhythemwand. I need its touch." The priest spoke from such deep need that T.K. did not question him, he just lurched to his feet and made his way passed Toto and out the door.

"I could have gotten your sword for you, priest," Ku'zn said angrily. "No need to make him go back out there."

"Not so," the priest whispered. "It is my hope he will retrieve more than a sword before the shadowbeast dies."

"It is not dead!" Ku'zn raced for the door.

"No, stop!" Shoutte commanded, "He must face this alone."

+++

The dust was not so thick yet that T.K. could not make out the shapes of tables, chairs, and the body. It was thick enough so that the bloodstains on the walls were rendered invisible. T.K. liked that.

Crystal from the skylight crunched underfoot and eddies of' debris bumped gently against the faint blue aura T.K. could now see around himself. At last he reached the creature, which lay on its side with Rhythemwand stuck completely through its stomach.

It lay unmoving.

He felt a shudder of revulsion when his fingers closed around the sword hilt and then twisted the blade to break the suction and draw it out of the body.

The shadowbeast shuddered and rolled on its back. T.K. jumped up with the sword ready to ward off an attack but the shadowbeast would never rise again.

Instead, a massive convulsion passed through the hideous form and it began to change.

"Oh my God!" T.K. murmured.

The creature's eyes were suddenly open. They were no longer the feral eyes of an animal—they were the innocent brown eyes of a child.

"Tee-Kay," Zulla whispered, looking up at him from the floor. "I hurt."

She was naked, her right shoulder gashed, a dozen minor bruises and cuts on her unblemished skin and a gaping hole in her stomach left by Rhythemwand.

"Why do I hurt?" She coughed and spit up blood.

T.K. dropped the sword and knelt beside her, holding her hand. As he did, a blue aura surrounded her to keep out the Z'last. "Oh, Zulla, Pumpkin, what have I done?"

"I had a nightmare again," she gently squeezed his hand. "It was red and black at the first and then it was so bright it hurt my eyes. You were there."

T.K. was crying, watching the bayonet flash in the depths of her eyes, listening to the M16 fire, feeling the bullets rip into his foot. "Oh God, Pumpkin."

"You were there," she continued in a voice that was losing life. "And you were beside me and you held me and it was all right."

He bent to cradle her head in his hands and watched the knife he saw reflected in her eyes dissolve. "Yes, it's alright, Pumpkin. I am holding you."

Her breathing was labored. Her whole lower body was soaked in blood.

"I'm going to die now," she said after a time.

"No, Pumpkin. No!"

"It's alright. I'm not alone. You're here." She was quiet for a time. "Am I really pretty?"

He could barely see her through his tears. He bent and kissed her lips as if they might shatter from his touch. "You're beautiful, Zulla."

"I'm happy, Tee-Kay." She smiled. "I love you."

Then she was dead.

T.K. held her for a long time, sobbing quietly, then threw his head back and yelled in a voice that dwarfed the fury of the storm. "I hate this stinking world too!"

Chapter Fourteen

"That which does not destroy me makes me pissed."
T.K. Mitchell (after a drunken brawl with Nitzche).

T.K. had been drunk for five days straight in an attempt to kill himself with excess, but it hadn't worked. And the hangover was proportional to his effort. During his binge the Assassin and Ku'zn had discovered Zul's body, swinging from a sconce where he had hung himself in despair, and some papers, which explained much.

"Zul had evidently been in the employ of Roosuf in Mephistal," Lord Shoutte whispered to T.K. "and when a prize vorn was crippled through Zul's neglect, the Wizard-Emperor shadow-cursed Zulla as revenge. The girl unknowingly killed her own mother. Zul fled here in hopes of controlling the curse."

T.K. was sipping tea at the kitchen counter. "Balls," the earthman mumbled into his mug. "Big hairy Kong balls."

Even whispered conversation made his head pound, so he concentrated on the teacup instead.

"I can give you thodist leaf for the pain in your head, Tee-Kay," Shoutte offered.

"No thanks, Erique. It helps me forget the pain in my gut, you know?"

"Yes, friend, I know."

"The team is hitched up," Ku'zn announced as she entered the room. She wore only a leather kilt and a necklace made from something she called sea worm tusk, which left her luxuriously furred breasts invitingly displayed.

T.K. glanced up at her display and felt a distant stir of lust. *Apparently I'm not dead yet*, he thought. *Damn it!*

"The pyres are ready as well," Conkull added as he entered. He too had spent several days in drunken depression over Rayjol's death but his Krinarian constitution made a hangover a rare occurrence.

"Come, priest," he said to Shoutte, "Words must be said, the fires lit, and then we must be away." The barbarian crouched, gathered Shoutte up into his arms like a child, and lifted him off his sleeping pallet.

"Careful you don't open his belly wound or I'll open your Krinarian hide," Ku'zn scolded.

"Have no fear, Erique," she added, "I will bring Rhythemwand."

"Ready to go?" she asked T.K, leaning over so her breasts dangled in his face. "I've put the tvek in the wagon."

"Have a heart, Peachfuzz," T.K. said, *You could put an eye out with one of those if I'm lucky*, he added to himself. "I'm coming." He pushed himself off the counter and climbed shakily to his feet with the aid of his walking stick.

"Okay," he said, "lead on, Macfuzz." Then he took a step and would have toppled over had not the Z'n scooped him up in her arms. "Husky broad, aren't you?" he said.

"You're not much heavier than I recall my brother being," she said, "and I used to pick him up and throw him across the hut."

"Well, still lucky for you I've been puking all day. I'm heavier on a full tank."

Outside the dead were waiting: Kwa Chun, Axe, Mace, Skins, Sword, Lance, Chain, Knife, Adrianna, Jonzun, Olzen, Orancha, Rayjol, Zul, and little Zulla.

More than a baker's dozen of death lined up on pyres of scavenged wood on the hill overlooking the entrance to Dragonthroat.

Before the pyres stood their survivors: Kwa Tzen and his son Kwa Chen, both still in deep shock, Lunit, Yomi, Tannilee, Conkull, the Assassin, Lee Zan Kar, Lord Shoutte, in his ceremonial robes, and T.K. leaning on Ku'zn.

Each said their goodbyes in turn.

Shoutte whispered the words of a truth chant in remembrance, Conkull mumbled an oath to Kron, and Lunit sang a bawdy ballad that Adrianna had taught her, accompanied by Yomi on the lyre.

The Assassin surprised everyone by performing a ritual sword salute for the dead. She then turned to Shoutte.

"My husband is dead. Vengeance is dead, and I live because you have honor, priest of the Kova. Be free of Shadows." So saying, she left a puzzled group, mounted her vorn and rode off.

T.K. placed a sketch of a rose he had drawn in the hands of Zulla's corpse. "Graceful stem, too soon snapped," he said. "Even thorns have a purpose and red can be a pretty color. Bye Pumpkin."

The pyres were all lit, the wood and dung-fed flames crackled, and Yomi's delicate hands played a rising song to the smoky ascent of their friends.

A little time later all were ready to leave, but not all were leaving as they planned. "But you must accompany me to the capital," Tannilee commanded Conkull. "You are sworn to my service."

"I was sworn to serve that good and noble man who goes to Kron. You are a spoiled brat, and I am a reiver who has better things to do than nursemaid you."

The barbarian mounted a vorn and gathered up the reins of a laden pack-vorn beside it, while the princess fumed in vain.

"You can't do that," she moaned. "I am the Princess of Cosen. Do you hear me?" she yelled for all to hear, "Stop him, I command it."

Everyone ignored her.

"Take care, big guy," T.K. called up to the barbarian, "and watch the feet next time." Conkull smiled.

"May your sword be always sharp, your purse full, and your companion beautiful, warp orphan," the barbarian said. "Farewell." He gave spur to his vorn and he was gone.

I could get that guy work back home if he could do an Austrian accent, T.K. noted. He climbed up on the driver's seat of the caravan wagon beside Yomi and picked up the reins. He dropped them again when he heard a familiar female voice from near the wagon.

"Thank the Lady, Teel Kantos, you are unharmed." It was Meegana Rakkdon. The old warp wizardess had stepped out of a warp a few feet away from the wagon.

"Jeez! Stop doing that," T.K. stared down at the frail old woman with the powerful voice and laughed. "Can't you start out as a floating bubble or something so I can see you coming?"

"There is urgency, Teel Kantos," Meegana insisted, "I fear that Roosuf has dispatched his chief executioner, in addition to the Z'last by which he forced you to this inn."

"Forced me, huh?" T.K. asked, "That bastard knew about Zulla."

Yomi, who had sat quietly while this exchange went on, could no longer contain herself.

"Tee-Kay," Yomi asked, "who is this woman?"

"Oh, 'scuse me. Yomi, meet Meegana Rakkdon. Meegana, this is Yomi." Ku'zn, who rounded the wagon in time to hear the exchange of names, stopped in her tracks and growled.

"Meegana Rakkdon," Ku'zn hissed, "The Mephan warpcrafter?"

"I am she, Z'n warrior," Meegana said calmly, "though I am here only in craft image, so you may sheath your anger."

"What are you doing here warp woman," Lord Shoutte called out through the wagon window, "and how is it you know her, Tee-Kay?"

"Easy, guys," T.K. said quickly, "I can explain."

At that moment, of course, Princess Tannilee rounded the wagon, marched straight up to T.K. "You savage, I want my wagon team hitched up right now and someone to drive it or I'll have to vorn-whip you."

"In the first place, you'll have to take a number," T.K. said. "In the second place, I doubt you can lift a vorn, and thirdly, your attendant and his son are coming with us to that healer's retreat where we're taking Erique. There's nobody left to drive you."

Tannilee took the news of this final desertion like the princess that she was: she screamed and lunged for T.K.'s throat.

Ku'zn got between the two of them and held Tannilee kicking off the ground by her shoulders, shaking her until she was quiet.

"I await an explanation," Shoutte said insistently. "How do you know this woman, Tee-Kay?"

"Well, uh—" T.K. began, "It's like this…"

"I must trust you all with a great secret," Meegana injected, "for I have no choice. My powers are limited here, and danger is very close at hand. This warp orphan is Teel Kantos, son of Sphona, who was daughter to Kantos, the Twenty Third Emperor of Mephan and the Mephastal Empire."

Everyone looked stunned. T.K. tried very hard to shrink and blow away.

"An heir?" Shoutte whispered.

"An emperor?" Tannilee giggled.

"A Mephistalian!" Ku'zn growled.

"Now wait a minute, Peachfuzz, honey," T.K. jumped down from the wagon seat to look directly into Ku'zn's eyes. "I've had no part in anything these Mepan boogers have done. I swear. I buried my heart at Wounded Knee, too. I didn't even know this mudball existed before I wound up here."

Ku'zn set the princess down and stared at the earthman, trying to reconcile her memories of him with her memories of the Mephistal raiders who slaughtered her blood mother.

"See what you've done," T.K. said to Meegana's image. "You can take your emperorship and shove ..."

"I seek the impostor heir!" A voice colder than the grave assaulted the group. They all turned as one to see the death black silhouette of Lord Gavilon on his war vorn, cresting a small rise one hundred yards across the flat plain in front of Dragonthroat's wind maze.

"I, Lord Gavilon, Servant of Roosuf of Mephan claim the right of challenge to this usurper. Surrender him and you may go with your lives. Fail to do so and you die."

"Quickly, Teel Kantos." Meegana insisted, "you flee until I can find aid for you; you cannot be harmed or the revolt will fail." T.K. kicked the wagon with his metal foot and cursed.

"That tears it." He turned to Meegana, "I've had it up to here with being manipulated from one place to another. And now you say run like a rabbit from a tinplated punk who works for the man who got Zulla into all this mess. No way!" He reached up into the driver seat and retrieved his walking stick. "Come on, Fred," he said to the stick, "let's go see about this 'Surrender Dorothy' crap!"

He started to walk away from the wagon and the startled group around it but decided to say something profound first. "If I don't come back, people, it's been a slice." He then went on while the others tried to figure out what he had said.

He stood on one side of the flat sandy clearing facing the hundred-yard distant Gavilon. "Okay, Mr. Bozo," T.K. yelled. "I'm the one you want, but you've picked the wrong day to get me ticked off." He looked over at the dark clouds of smoke rising off the pyres above Dragonthroat. "So let's get this nonsense over with."

Gavilon remained a statue on his vorn, his black armor soaking in the suns' light and giving back nothing. He drew a black crystal blade from a scabbard of human skin and held it aloft. "I will bring your head to my liege lord, so I have sworn."

Then Gavilon charged; a black juggernaut of man and vorn united, sword and antler points to one purpose—the death of T. K. Mitchell.

The group of Dragonthroat survivors watched helpless in terror as the fully armored knight bore down on their friend. T.K. was 'ferociously' attired in a Mickey Mouse t-shirt, buckskin pants, and moccasins. They all knew with certainty that T.K. had chosen to commit suicide.

Ku'zn made to move forward but Lord Shoutte stopped her with the words, "This is a fight he must make alone, the Rhythem led him to this moment."

The great black charger with its emissary of death bore down on him relentlessly, great sprays of sand flying in a wake behind the vorn's hooves. The earthman stood placid, his arms at his sides, his walking stick held in a relaxed grip at his right side and whistled Darth Vader's theme from Star Wars.

He is mad, Gavilon thought in the part of his consciousness still fascinated by the ways of those who felt emotion. *The* fear *has driven him to throw his life away!* The war vorn thundered toward the lone man with the inevitable fury of a tidal wave, yet T.K. stood like a sand castle, seemingly uncaring at his eminent washout.

This placid acceptance of the inevitable began to prey more and more on the mind of Gavilon. At the last three yards from the earthman, the warrior-wraith reined his mount to a halt.

"You crave the release of death so much you would greet it with no protest?" Gavilon asked with the voice of the grave. His impatient mount sidestepped closer to T.K. so that by the time the earthman replied the two men were just out of sword length.

"I came here to kick your ass as therapy, schmuck," T.K. whispered. "Let's get to it."

Lord Gavilon felt emotion at that moment: hate for this usurper, for his strength, for his acceptance, and for the ability to feel pain, which must have inspired such bravado. It made Gavilon tingle to anticipate the joy he would feel when he heard Teel Kantos' skull crack like a nut beneath his vorn's hooves.

Lord Gavilon pulled back on the reins and his vorn reared up its front legs, kicking violently in a well-rehearsed war move.

T.K. watched the vorn rear up from his relaxed and distant mind-place, the place he went when violence was eminent, and calculated his options: *avoid till exhaustion overtakes me, retreat until I find better ground or he runs me down, or I can attack.*

All these thoughts were thought in less time than it took for the vorn to reach the height of its arch. At that instant, as fast as thought, T.K. made his choice: attack!

With perfect textbook technique, the earthman stepped in toward the vorn with his left foot (leaning his face away from the razor hooves) and snapped his right leg into a sidekick. His duralumin foot hit the animal with a calculated blow, right above the center of gravity, and sent it staggering back.

He immediately followed with a second kick to the same spot. That proved too much for the animal's balance. One great bleat of terror and the vorn fell directly backward, crushing the struggling Lord Gavilon beneath its bulk.

The vorn rolled to its feet quickly and pranced off to a comfortable distance, confused by what had just occurred. Lord Gavilon lay on his caved in side, his crushed armor marking the extent of his wounds, and tried to understand what had just happened.

All he could absorb was the certain knowledge that he was dying. That awakened an emotion in him he had never felt before: fear. The feeling was intense and stark, painful and exhilarating. In his last moments the Lord High Executioner envied all he had ever killed for having experienced this feeling before him.

T.K. leapt quickly back as the hind legs of the vorn kicked up as it fell. He went immediately into fighting stance but just as quickly realized it was unnecessary. He relaxed and walked up to the fallen man, removing the dark helm to expose the pasty face, now flushed with waning life. T.K. looked into the fading eyes and saw an unasked question in them.

The earthman thought for a second and then smiled evilly at the dying Gavilon. "And your little dog, too!" T.K. said.

Lord Gavilon died puzzled.

T.K. limped back to his amazed friends a little annoyed that one of the flailing back hooves of the vorn had stuck him soundly on his right calf. When he arrived back at the wagon no one spoke while he mounted to the driver's seat.

"All right, Meg," T.K. said, "we'll talk about me starting this revolution of yours, but it's only to pay back this Roosuf dude. I'm telling you in advance, I don't want the job."

The image of Meegana smiled cunningly. "We shall see when the time comes. For now, travel to Tolan. I will greet you there." The image faded and was gone.

"Well," T.K. said, "I guess it's time we get this show on the road. All aboard for the Tolan Express."

Ku'zn looked up at the earthman with a crooked grin on her face. "You and my brother would get along well, even if you are a Mephistalian."

"I dig you too, Peachfuzz."

"As I have said before of you, my friend," Lord Erique Shoutte whispered. "Inspired and somewhat insane."

"Guess I'll be hangin' out on Altiva awhile, Erique. Even though it's not my planet, monkeyboy. My throne awaits!" He bellowed with a sudden gusto.

"What about me?" Tannilee's pitiful voice injected.

"You know how it is, doll," the earthman said with fiendish delight. "Affairs of state, and all that." He tapped on the wagon. "Buckle up folks, we're on our way to visit my newfound relatives."

"You are a very interesting man, Tee-Kay," Yomi said beside him, "I am sure your relatives will be equally so."

"I'll make you my minister of morals, hon," T.K. said, "God knows I need one."

"What about me?" Tannilee was near tears. "I must get to the palace before my father learns I deserted the tutor he sent me too study with."

"Sorry, doll," T.K. said in an affected Bronx accent, "Teamsters Union rules say no hitchhikers." He grabbed the reins.

"Please, my father will be angry if I don't get back." She whined.

T.K. smiled. "You said the magic word, sweet cheeks: please. Hop on board—but remember our motto: 'Ass or grass, nobody rides for free.'"

When she was aboard T.K. glanced up the hill to where the pyres were, blew a final kiss to Zulla, and then began to sing, "We're off to see the wizard" as he urged the team forward on the long road to the throne.

Like it or not, T.K. Mitchell had at last come home.

THE BEGINNING...

Dedication:

To Jane McNulty Pulver who first believed in me and Altiva and to ET who continues to believe and amaze me every day.

ABOUT OUR CREATORS

WRITER

TEEL JAMES GLENN - has stories have been printed in magazines from *Weird Tales, Spinetingler, SciFan, Mad, Black Belt, Fantasy Tales, Pulp Empire, Sherlock Holmes Mystery, SciFan, Sixgun Western, Crimson Streets, Silver Blade Quarterly, Tales of Old, Blazing Adventures* and scores of other publications and dozens of books and anthologies in many genres. His short story "The Clockwork Nutcracker" won best steampunk story for 2013 from Preditor and Editors poll.

He is also the winner of the Pulp Factory award for Best novel (A Cowboy in Carpathia) and the 2012 Pulp Ark Award for Best Author, his website is: TheUrbanSwashbuckler.com

INTERIOR ILLUSTRATOR

CHRIS NYE - has been a graphic artist and illustrator for over 30 years. He has actively worked in the comic book and graphic novel industry since 2001. In addition to work for Airship 27 Productions, he is currently working on comic book projects for Sitcomics and Markosia. He is also a graphic artist, illustrator and writer with Lockheed Martin. He resides in Simpsonville, South Carolina.

COVER ARTIST

ROB DAVIS - began his professional art career doing illustrations for role-playing games in the late 1980s. Not long after he began lettering and inking, then penciling comics for a number of small black and white comics publishers. Most notably Rob worked for Eternity Comics (which eventually became Malibu Comics in the 1990s) on their book SCIMIDAR with writer R.A. Jones. Branching out to other black and white publishers and eventually working at both DC and Marvel Rob worked on likeness intensive comics like TV adaptations of QUANTUM LEAP and STAR TREK's many incarnations mostly on the DEEP SPACE NINE comics for Malibu. At Marvel he worked on the Saturday morning cartoon adaptation PIRATES OF DARK WATER. After the comics industry implosion in the late 1990s Rob picked up work on video games, advertising illustration and T-shirt design as well as some small press comics like ROBYN OF SHERWOOD for Caliber.

Rob continues to do the occasional self-published comic book and as publisher and designer for his small-press production REDBUD STUDIO COMICS. As well look for Kickstarter fundraisers for his work with SILVERLINE COMICS on TWILIGHT GRIMM with writer R.A. Jones. Rob is Art Director, Designer and Illustrator for the New Pulp production outfit AIRSHIP 27 partnered with writer/editor Ron Fortier.

Rob is the two time recipient of the PULP FACTORY AWARD for "Best Interior Illustrations" since 2010 for his work on SHERLOCK HOLMES: CONSULTING DETECTIVE. He works and lives in central Missouri with his wife, two children and soon to be first granddaughter.

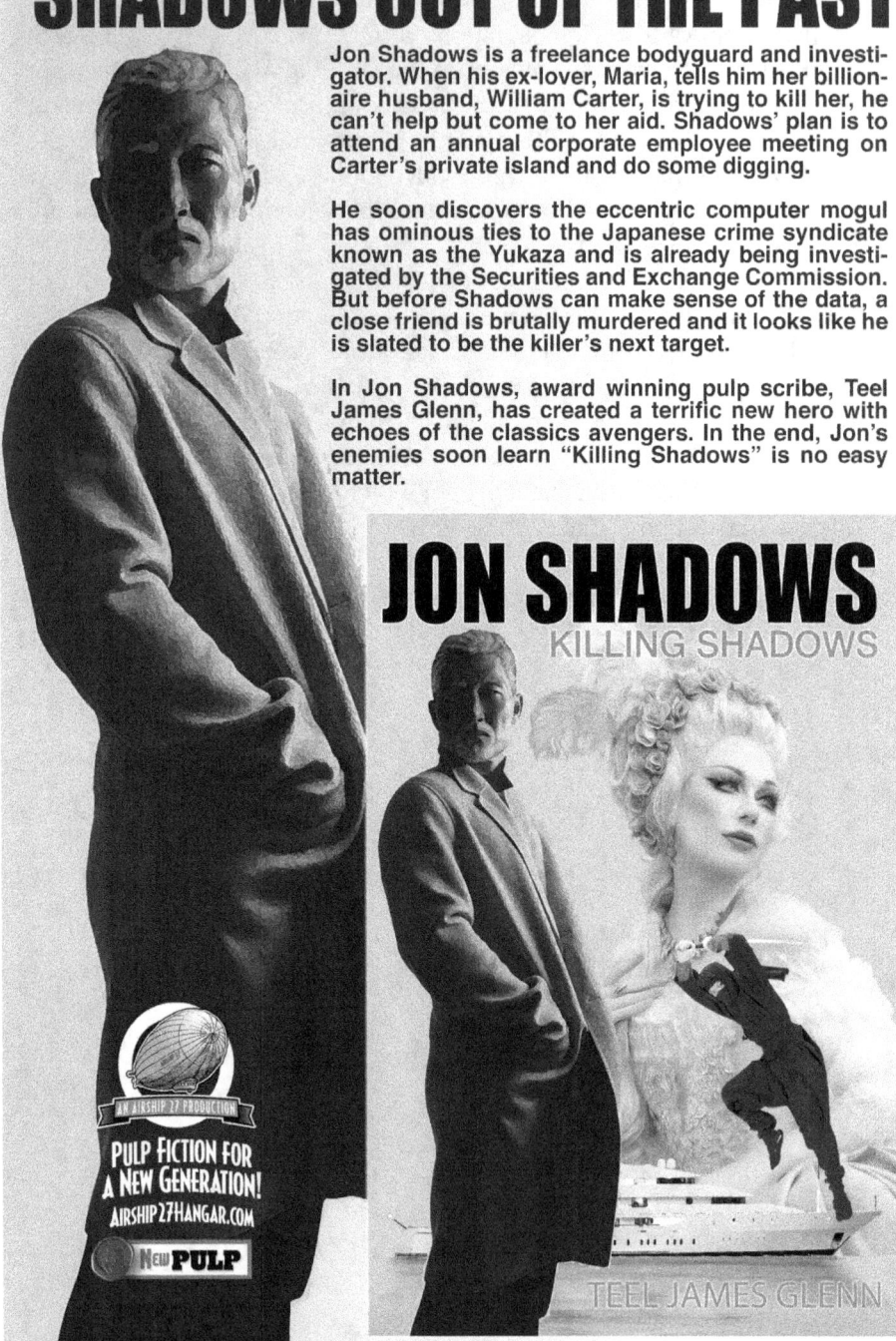